THE SILVER HAND

THE SILVER HAND

TERRY DEARY

BLOOMSBURY EDUCATION
LONDON OXFORD NEW YORK NEW DELHI SYDNEY

BLOOMSBURY EDUCATION
Bloomsbury Publishing Plc
50 Bedford Square, London, WC1B 3DP, UK

BLOOMSBURY, BLOOMSBURY EDUCATION and the Diana logo are trademarks of
Bloomsbury Publishing Plc

First published in Great Britain 2018 by Bloomsbury Publishing Plc

A catalogue record for this book is available from the British Library

ISBN: PB: 978-1-4729-2948-8; ePDF: 978-1-4729-2950-1; ePub: 978-1-4729-2949-5

2 4 6 8 10 9 7 5 3 1

Typeset by Newgen KnowledgeWorks Pvt. Ltd., Chennai, India
Printed and bound by CPI Group (UK) Ltd, Croydon, CR0 4YY

All papers used by Bloomsbury Publishing Plc are natural, recyclable products from wood
grown in well managed forests. The manufacturing processes conform to the environmental
regulations of the country of origin

To find out more about our authors and books visit www.bloomsbury.com
and sign up for our newsletters

All the quotes at the beginning of chapters are by the Roman writer and orator, Cicero, who lived between 106 BC and 43 BC.

Chapter One

'The enemy is within the gates'

21 March 1918: Bray, Northern France

Aimee sped down the lane, her pigtail streaming out behind her. Dust clouds swirled up as her boots flew over the stony cart track and the cows near the hedges shied away. A mist hung over the fields and crept through the streets and wrapped itself around the chimneys like a scarf. The distant drumming of the thousands of guns to the east sounded louder and closer this morning.

Aimee skidded as she turned into the school gates and she tumbled through the door into the cool, dark hallway. The school cat, the colour of rust and ashes, jumped up from its seat outside the school office.

She threw open the classroom door and stood gasping to get her breath back. Master DuPont glared at her, his hand that held the chalk frozen in the air and his face as sour as green plums. 'Aimee Fletcher, you are late.'

Aimee nodded and panted. 'Yes, but...'

'*Again*. What is it this time? Did your hen get its head stuck in the wire of the chicken shed? Or was it the cow today, kicking over the milk bucket? You have a different excuse every day. Maybe you found a mermaid in the horse trough and stopped for a chat?'

'No, sir, but...'

'You have been late three times this week and you must be punished.' The teacher picked up a small book covered in green leather. 'You will take this book by Cicero, the great Roman writer. You will stay behind after school and turn his wise Latin words into French.'

Aimee's nut-brown face turned bright red. 'Oh, I'll like that.'

The teacher closed his tired eyes and sighed softly. 'You will, too,' he murmured.

'I love Latin,' Aimee went on. 'I lie in bed at night and tell myself the old folk tales but I change the words into Latin for fun. The big bad wolf is *lupus maximus malam...*'

'I know that,' the teacher snapped. 'Now sit at your desk. We have just started an English lesson.'

'That's not as much fun as Latin,' Aimee argued.

Master DuPont gripped the chalk so hard it cracked and the white dust floated through a morning sunbeam. 'The British soldiers are our friends. They are fighting against the Germans who invaded our land, our own big bad wolves. We must be polite to the British and, when we see them marching through our village, we must speak to them in English.'

Aimee spread her hands. 'My dad is English... though he's joined the French army... I can speak it very well already.'

The teacher put the broken chalk down on his desk and rubbed his weary eyes. 'I am sure you can, Aimee Fletcher. You are the best pupil in Latin *and* English in the class.'

'And history,' Aimee put in.

'And history.' The teacher nodded. 'But you *must* learn to be on time. You will stay behind after school today and translate some Cicero.'

Aimee shuffled from one foot to the other. 'But, sir, that's what I was *trying* to tell you... there won't *be* any more school.'

Some of the children giggled. Aimee was mad. No more school? What next? No more sun in the sky? No more River Somme at the end of the road?

Master DuPont glared at her. 'What do you mean?'

'I can't say. The younger children would panic.'

'Aimee Fletcher, if you are making up some story to escape punishment then I can tell you...'

'*Intus est hostis*,' she hissed.

The teacher blinked. 'Cicero?'

Aimee nodded. 'Yes... so the young ones aren't scared. *Intus est hostis*.'

But then the teacher did just what Aimee hoped he wouldn't do. He said the Latin words in French.

'The enemy is within the gates? You mean the Germans are coming?'

Aimee groaned. The younger children gasped and whimpered and panicked. A shiver from the trembling pupils seemed to chill the room. Little Marie Picard screamed and pointed at the glass in the classroom door. Everyone's eyes followed her finger.

A soldier was standing outside.

21 March 1918: Saint Quentin, Northern France

Marius Furst stepped out of the trench and looked to the west. A mild breeze blew in the boy's face and carried the smell of stale death into his nostrils. But it didn't disturb the fog of the spring morning or the thunder of the heavy guns in the battles ahead of him. 'So this is no man's land?' he asked.

The soldier with a face of flint gave a laugh as sharp as a dog's bark. 'Never seen it before, lad?'

'I've never been near the trenches before. I just left Germany to help us win the war.'

The soldier had a stripe on his arm that showed he was a corporal. 'You look too young to fight.'

'Yes. No,' Marius mumbled. 'My grandmother taught me about herbs and healing. I thought I could work in the hospitals.'

'But they let you join the army?' the corporal asked. 'They gave you a uniform.'

'No. I met a soldier on the road. He was running away... a deserter. He swapped clothes with me.'

The soldier nodded his head and a dark fringe of hair flopped over his eyes; pale eyes that glowed bright. He had a tiny moustache like a small paintbrush. 'We need more brave lads like you... and fewer of the cowards that run from the fight. If they were all like you – and me – we'd have won this war years ago.' He patted Marius on the shoulder. 'Brave lad.'

'I don't want to kill anyone – just help our injured countrymen. I've seen a few that came home wounded.'

'Just a few? Then you're lucky,' the soldier said. 'I've been in and out of these trenches for four years and seen things that will haunt me for the rest of my life.'

'What sort of things?' Marius asked, wide-eyed and pale.

The man just shook his head. 'It's over now. This trench war is over. We're moving west. We're moving fast. We'll drive the British into the sea and send them back to their puny little island. Four years of mud and blood and we're on the move at last. They're running away like trench rats,' he snorted.

Marius stepped forward. 'I'd better get after them. The hospital is packed and ready to follow our great army.'

The soldier just nodded. 'They say we drove the British back fifteen kilometres yesterday. Get your running boots on, lad.' He hefted a pack on to his bony shoulder, gripped his rifle and headed to the road where lorries full of soldiers trundled westwards.

'See you,' Marius called after him.

The man turned and scowled. 'I hope not. If I see you then it means I'll be wounded in hospital. I've been there once and don't want to see you nurses again.'

Marius grinned. 'I suppose so, Corporal.'

The soldier stared towards the sinking sun in the west. His pale eyes glowed icicle-blue. 'When we have beaten the British we'll take their empire, then crush the French and rule the world.'

Marius blinked. 'You think so?'

The soldier sniffed the rank, dank air. 'I know so... or my name isn't Hitler. Adolf Hitler.' He turned on his heel and marched off.

Marius picked up his own pack of bandages, potions and pills and set off over no man's land. For four years this ground between the British trenches and the German trenches had been gashed and gouged, shaped, scraped and scored by shells from the big guns. The boy knew the sour smell of the killing ground from the bodies and the clothes of the soldiers he'd patched up, back in the Saint Quentin hospital.

He stepped carefully on to the softened soil. In the watery shell-holes there was a green metal-sheen of slime made by the poison gases the armies had fired at one another.

New grass was already beginning to grow over the ruined earth and, high above him, a skylark sang. It seemed to sing what the soldier had said: 'It's over now, it's over now.' Marius walked another hundred metres and reached the trenches that had just been deserted by the British. This was where men had crouched below their sandbags and had burrowed shelters into the sides of the trenches.

The boy stepped down on to the damp boards of the trench and peered into one of the dugouts. The mud walls were lined with old waterproof capes and pieces of boxwood. A crate made a table and the enemy had found a shabby old horsehair chair to sit on.

A soot-black kettle sat on a rusting paraffin stove, its water cold as Christmas now. Marius shook his head at the misery the British had suffered here. No wonder they had fled down the road home. The German trenches – the ones he'd seen a hundred metres away – were dug deep and snug.

He felt brighter after what that little corporal had said. He stepped back into the evening air and turned west to catch up with his troops who were striding forward and driving the British like cattle before them. Marius whistled a tune of a song from an earlier war...

'Dear Fatherland, no fear be thine, dear Fatherland, no fear be thine, Firm and true stands the Watch, the Watch at the Rhine.'

He hurried through the evening air and his heavy pack now felt light as a butterfly. 'Firm and true, that's me. Firm and true.'

21 March 1918: Bray

There was a clatter and a rattle of tumbling chairs as a dozen children fled to the corner of the room. Aimee sighed. The number of children in Bray school had fallen since the war started – now there were only enough to make a single class – and she was the oldest. Sometimes she felt like a mother hen to the little chicks.

The soldier tapped on the glass and opened the door. Master DuPont swallowed so hard his stiff collar creaked.

'Do you speak English?' the soldier asked, tugging off his cap and tucking it under his arm.

The teacher stared and his mouth opened but no sound came out. The whimpering children fell silent.

'I speak English,' Aimee said quietly. Then she turned to her classmates. 'It's all right. He's British. He's a friend. Go back to your seats.' The children slipped back shy as smoke and watched wide-eyed.

For four years they had lived with the distant trembling of the mighty war guns to the east. Most of the younger ones still had nightmare memories of the days, back in 1914, when the Germans had arrived and taken over their homes. They remembered the hard-faced, stone-faced, grey-faced men with bayonets glinting in the sun.

They remembered hiding in their cellars as the British army swept in from the west and drove the invaders back. And back. And further back. And then the armies stopped. They faced one another in trenches dug into the soft soils near the River Somme.

The children heard stories of how the armies put up barbed wire between themselves and their enemies then tried to smash the trenches opposite with the great guns that made the Bray school walls shiver.

Sometimes the guns fell silent but the village was never free of the motor-lorries and wagons drawn by sweating horses. They were like a circus passing through the town as they pulled supplies to their tired army and their hungry horses. It was a carnival train of shells and bullets, cannon and tanks, wood and wire and gas masks and grenades. A daily carnival of death.

The traffic snarled and snaggled in the narrow village streets, where it met with traffic going the other way: the marching men and the wounded, bandaged soldiers that were being carried to Amiens or back home to Britain.

Master DuPont found his voice. 'How can I help, sir?' he asked.

'Good morning, I am Captain Ellis.' The young soldier had a kindly face under the dust from the roads. The children watched, agape, though they didn't understand much of what he said. He went on, 'The British army needs to take over your school. We want a command base for General Bruce.'

Master DuPont blew out his cheeks. 'The general can't command the army from here,' he argued. 'The trenches are twenty or thirty kilometres away.'

The soldier sighed. 'Not any longer. The enemy has broken through our lines. They smashed us with thousands of shells then marched over no man's land under cover of the fog. The Germans are coming.'

Aimee smiled and spread her hands wide. 'I told you,' she said to the teacher.

Master DuPont's face turned cloud-grey. 'The children will have to leave. They'll have to go to Amiens. There are homes waiting for them there. We never thought we'd see this day.'

Aimee whispered the news to the children and they gathered their pencils and books and got ready to exit the classroom. The teacher watched them and despair ran through the wrinkles of his old face. 'What will I do?' he groaned.

'Give me the keys to the school,' Captain Ellis said.

Master DuPont reached into the desk and passed a tarnished set of clanking keys to the captain. He looked at the children and tried to smile. 'Wherever you go, my young ones, remember you are French and our spirit shall never be defeated. Let us sing our anthem one last time before you leave.'

Captain Ellis stood to attention. Aimee stepped across to the piano in the corner of the room and struck the notes firmly. The quavering voices of the children filled the room.

'Arise, children of the Fatherland,
The day of glory has arrived!
Against us tyranny's
bloody banner is raised.
Let's march, let's march!

*Let an impure blood
soak our fields!'*

Aimee finished with a crashing chord that shook the windows. Master DuPont sniffed and blew his nose loudly. 'God speed and prosper you in all you do,' he said.

The teacher lowered his head and walked out of the door into the misty air without looking back, and Aimee suddenly saw the fearsome old man was frail as dead leaves.

21 March 1918: Amiens, Northern France

Brass buttons shone and medal ribbons were a rainbow of colour on the drab uniforms of the officers who sat and stared at the map on the wall. There were enough moustaches in the room to make a yard brush and the lips underneath them were tightly turned down when they heard the grim news.

General Bruce stood in front of the map with a pointer. 'We knew the German army was going to launch Operation Michael against us but I didn't think they'd get so far so quickly.' He turned to a small man with a uniform as neat as a needle. 'What went wrong, Colonel Wright?'

Wright stepped forward and took a pencil to point at the map. 'The morning was foggy. The Germans hit us with thirty divisions in the first wave. When the fog lifted, no man's land was swarming with horses and men. They had rifles and "potato-masher" stick grenades. Their shells hit our trenches, which were soon filled with dead or wounded. The British men left alive were ready to surrender.'

General Bruce shook his head. 'A dark day. The enemy drove through our trenches and on for eight miles. We have to stand and fight somewhere.'

A sergeant was standing by the door and there was a murmur of talk as someone passed him a sheet of paper. The sergeant had cropped dark hair and the eyes of a hawk, over a thin nose and a cruel mouth. But the strangest thing that caught your eye was his shining left hand. It was silver. A false hand taking the place of one he'd lost.

The man with the silver hand held up the paper in his right hand. 'Excuse me, General Bruce. It's a message from General Haig.'

'Not now, Sergeant Grimm,' Colonel Wright snapped.

'Sorry, sir. It's important,' the sergeant said. He marched over to General Bruce as stiff as a puppet and handed him the paper.

Bruce looked up and said to his officers, 'Go back to your men and read them a copy of this message.'

'What does it say, sir?' Colonel Wright asked.

General Bruce read it quietly. '*Today the enemy began his terrific attacks against us. Many amongst us are now tired. To those I would say that Victory will belong to the side which holds out the longest. The French army is moving quickly and in great numbers to help us. We have no choice, we must fight it out. Every yard must be held to the last man: there must be no retreat. With our backs to the wall we must fight on to the end. The safety of our homes and the Freedom of mankind are in our hands right now.*'

Colonel Wright nodded. 'With our backs to the wall.'

One of the officers asked, 'Where is our wall? Where do we stop them?'

The general pointed to the map. 'Here,' he said and drew a line on the map. It passed through the village of Bray. 'Sergeant Grimm will take the orders to our troops,' he said, nodding towards the man with the silver hand.

'Can we stop them?' a young captain asked.

'We *can* stop them. Then we will drive them all the way back to Germany,' the general said with a sly smile. 'You see, we have a new weapon that will win the war. It is so secret hardly anyone outside this room knows about it.'

A shiver of excitement ran through the officers. 'Are you going to tell us about this new weapon?' the captain asked. 'Is it a new tank? A new plane?'

General Bruce gave a wide smile under his moustache. 'A new sort of gas. DM gas. When it is fired at the enemy it will turn them into statues. I have the formula here,' he said and waved a brown envelope at the men in the room. He turned and handed it to the sergeant. 'Grimm?'

'Yes, sir?'

'Take this and lock it in my safe, then take a car to Bray. See that it's ready for us to set up a new base. Captain Ellis is already there and I'll be along tomorrow when I'm finished here. Help Captain Ellis till then.'

'Yes, sir,' Grimm said and his good right hand trembled a little as he took the envelope of secrets.

21 March 1918: Bray

The young children of Bray school hurried past the watch-cat at the door. Its tail swished, annoyed at the bustle and banging of those pupils fleeing school so early in the day. Aimee followed more slowly, then began to run down the street, the nails in her boots chiming on the cobbles. Everyone in the village looked as grey-faced as the morning mist. Grey with fear. Even the red-faced butcher, Mr Albert, had faded to pink.

Aimee turned into the dusty lane that led to her farm and the cows seemed restless as ripples on the River Somme. The rumble of the guns should have been muffled by the foggy air but it was louder, closer, more menacing now.

The girl ran into the cobbled courtyard where the washing on the line flapped against her face. Her mother was pegging Aimee's clean smock dresses to the line. Colette Fletcher was a strong woman, running the farm while her husband fought in the French army. Her dark hair had strands of grey in it and her pale eyes were calm and smiling. Aimee panted, 'The Germans really are coming.'

'The ribbon in your pigtail is coming loose,' Mrs Fletcher said.

'You *said* the Germans were coming, Maman. Before I left for school, you said. We'll have to move to Amiens. We'll have to leave the farm.'

Mrs Fletcher picked up the empty clothes basket and moved into the kitchen. 'We won't be going to Amiens,' she said.

'But...'

'The Germans will not hurt us. We are farmers. They need our land for their horses, our barns for their men, our eggs and cattle for their food. When the Germans were here four years ago they treated us well.'

Aimee had been so young back then. She had memories seen through a fog of time. 'They bombed us,' she said.

Mrs Fletcher laughed. 'No, our friends the *British* bombed us to drive the Germans out. And it worked. If the Germans get this far again they will treat us well.'

Aimee was soothed by her mother's gentle voice. She watched her put a log in the stove and heat another pan of water for the washtub. 'Maman... no one in the school knew the Germans were on their way. Not until a British Captain told them.'

Her mother didn't answer.

'But *you* knew. You knew before anyone in Bray. How did you know?'

Mrs Fletcher poured a cup of milk for her daughter and sat at the table. She was silent for a long time and finally said, 'Aimee, I am going to tell you a secret. It is so dangerous I really shouldn't. But... I want you to know in case the Germans do get as far as Bray. Then I may... I may do some strange things and I want you to understand why.'

Aimee shivered though the weak sunlight beamed through the dusty window and the stove hissing with logs made the kitchen warm. She waited. Finally Mrs Fletcher started to speak.

'The British and French armies have a team of spies. Not soldiers. Ordinary men and women living in France who want them to win this endless war. The group is known as the White Lady.'

'Are they led by a white lady?' Aimee asked.

'No. There is a story that one day the ghost of a woman, dressed in white, will appear. When she is seen it will mean the end of the German king's rule.'

'And are you one of the White Lady group? Are you a spy?' Aimee breathed. She had read stories about spies but in her mind they were men dressed in black, creeping through night-dark woods.

'In every village there are men and women waiting to serve our armies. If the Germans come to Bray, I'll report it to the British – I'll count how many troops and guns the enemy has. I'll report on where the soldiers are staying... where their railway lines are laid and what fields they are using to land their aircraft.'

Aimee's mouth went dry. 'The Germans would shoot you if they ever caught you doing that.'

Mrs Fletcher spread her hands. 'I'll just have to make sure I'm not caught then. The radio is well hidden in the barn.'

'I've never seen you talking on a radio,' Aimee said.

'I do it at midnight when you're asleep. The villages to the east have been reporting on the new enemy attacks. The Germans call it Operation Michael.'

Aimee's eyes brightened. 'That's how you knew they were on their way before anyone else in the village?'

Her mother nodded. 'Your father is fighting with rifles and bombs. I will fight using my eyes and ears.'

'And me?'

'You can go to Amiens, if you like. You have cousins there who'd take you in. You'd be safe there.'

Aimee had met her older cousins before the war. They treated her like a maid-servant and called her 'stupid peasant'.

'I want to stay,' she said.

Colette Fletcher grinned. 'And I want you to stay. The enemy would never think a schoolgirl could be carrying secret messages.'

'You'd let me carry messages for you?' A shadow crossed Aimee's face. 'If they caught me I would never betray you.'

'You wouldn't have to,' her mother said. She picked up a broom from the corner of the room. 'This is a magic broom.'

Aimee looked cross. 'Don't be silly. Magic is for fairy tales.'

'Maybe. But this broom holds a secret message that may help us win the war.'

Aimee frowned and picked it up. 'It's a broom,' she said. 'Stop teasing me, Maman.'

The girl had left the door of the kitchen open. A man's voice said, 'It is the broom of a White Lady.' And Aimee thought her heart had stopped.

21 March 1918: East of Peronne, Northern France

Marius Furst had walked eight weary kilometres before he came across a canteen at the side of the road. It was well away from the smoke-fogged street of houses. The ruined buildings had broken windows and cracking walls. They trembled with the roar of the guns. The boy joined a line of soldiers grumbling as they waited for the thin soup and black bread.

'Oh I wish I was back in my bakery,' a large man with a dust-covered face moaned. 'My bread is the best in Uttfeld.'

A skinny man beside him sneered. 'That was in the days before the war. When we had real flour... not this acorn powder.' He dipped the black crust in the soup and sucked on it.

The fat baker poked the skinny man in the chest. 'I could still get real flour... if I paid enough.'

'Yes and then charged us poor folk enough.'

'The baker's hand grabbed the little man's tunic and shook him. 'It's the farmers who grow the corn that make the money. Not me. It's the millers who grind it in their mills that are getting rich. Not us poor bakers.'

'I only said...'

'Well don't say anything, you worm.'

A sergeant stepped forward and slapped the baker's hand away from the little soldier. 'Save your fighting talk for the British or I'll have you charged. You'll be peeling potatoes for a week.'

Someone in the queue sniggered. 'What's a potato? I haven't seen one of them in years.'

The weary men laughed. 'Don't let Franz near any potatoes – he'd eat the lot, skins and all.'

Marius watched in wonder. He never dreamed the soldiers could squabble like foxes fighting over a chicken bone.

'If you've all finished your delicious soup, get back in the wagon,' said the sergeant. 'We'll be in Peronne tomorrow if you fight your way there. The Brits are running so fast they're leaving their supplies behind. By Saturday night you'll be feasting like King Wilhelm.'

The men gave a cheer and began to climb on the truck. 'Feasting like the king... if we're not shot first,' the skinny soldier grouched. The cheering died in the throats of the men.

'Or if the flu doesn't kill us,' a pale man in a worn and faded uniform wailed. His eyes were rimmed with red and his skin was shiny as wax. He gave a ratcheting cough and the men on the seats shuffled away from him. They were all aboard, the driver turned a starting handle and the engine gave an answering cough.

The sergeant looked back at Marius standing by the canteen. 'Come on, lad. Get aboard.'

'He's not one of ours, Sergeant,' someone said.

'Where are you headed?' the sergeant asked.

Marius glanced at the map he'd torn from a school atlas. 'A hospital... near Peronne.'

'Jump up, then.'

Marius was pulled up on to the crowded lorry as it popped and wheezed, rolled and groaned along the rutted road. The soldier in the faded uniform wheezed like the lorry. 'Hospital worker, eh? Can you cure the flu?'

Marius frowned. He knew his grandmother had a potion for fevers. 'I have a cure. Yes,' he said.

The men in the back of the lorry laughed. 'Then you're not a doctor – they don't have a cure, son. You are a magician. A miracle worker.'

The boy smiled shyly. The coughing soldier leaned towards him and his breath stank and stung Marius's nose like dragon smoke. 'Have you got something for *me*, lad?'

Marius reached into his backpack and pulled out a small brown glass bottle. He handed it over and said, 'A little sip...'

But the soldier had pulled out the cork and sucked on the bottle greedily. 'That's all I had,' Marius whispered.

The lorry trundled on and the men began to sing softly. A gloom-filled song of a soldier's girl who'd died of a fever.

'A long black coat, I must now wear.
A sorrow great, is what I bear.
A sorrow great and so much more,
My grief will last for evermore.'

As the sun sank in the west, and the amber sky turned to old bronze, the men fell silent and began to doze. Marius fell into a deep sleep, exhausted.

21 March 1918: Bray

Captain Ellis stood at the kitchen door of Mrs Fletcher's farmhouse and grinned at Aimee. 'Did I startle you? I'm sorry.'

The soldier took off his cap and strode across the room, holding out his hand to Mrs Fletcher. 'Colette Fletcher? I am Captain Ellis.'

Aimee's mother smiled warmly. 'We've spoken on the radio. It's good to meet you.' She turned to her daughter. 'Captain Ellis is a spy chief in the British army. He's my contact there.' She turned back to the soldier. 'Sit down. Have a glass of wine. I was just telling Aimee about the broomsticks.'

'Sounded like a fairy tale to me,' the girl grumbled, still annoyed because she felt she was being teased.

Captain Ellis sat down at the table as Colette Fletcher served him red wine in a stone flagon. 'The broom handles are hollow,' he explained. 'Our White Lady spies put beans inside the hollow handle to send us a message in code. Runner beans are the number of German soldiers in the area... three runner beans means there are three thousand men in Bray, for example. Haricot beans are the number of heavy guns the enemy have to attack us with, and so on.'

Aimee nodded. 'So then you know how many British soldiers and guns you need to fight against them?'

'Exactly. When the Germans get to Bray your mother will send messages to General Bruce in Amiens using the brooms and beans code.'

Aimee was shocked. '*When* the Germans get to Bray? You mean *if*?'

Captain Ellis leaned forward and lowered his voice. 'Your mother knows this – so it's not a great secret – but the enemy are attacking in great numbers and at great speed. It is best if we back off.'

'Run away?' the girl cried. 'Leave them to capture Bray?'

The soldier stayed calm. 'They are moving so fast they will leave their supplies far behind. By the end of the week they will have to stop and wait for food and bullets and hospitals to catch up. Especially the hospitals. We will pull our army back to Amiens. Then, when they are exhausted, we'll strike. We'll drive them all the way back to Germany.'

Aimee frowned. 'What do you mean, especially the hospitals?'

Captain Ellis gave a small smile. 'You're a bright girl, Aimee. What I mean is we have reports coming in from our White Lady spies to the east. The enemy hospitals are filling up... and so are their burial grounds.'

'Because you are shooting so many?'

'No. Because there is disease spreading through the German army. They are falling sick in their thousands with influenza – or flu.'

'Master DuPont, our teacher, had that last Christmas. He was off for three days and I had to teach the little ones,' Aimee said with a shrug. 'Then I was sick for a week.'

'Then you are lucky. This is a new type of flu. It is deadly, but if you've had it – and then got better – you won't catch it again.'

'But it's killing the Germans?'

'When their soldiers are crammed into the motor-lorries that carry them forward they are spreading it. A few recover. Many are dead in three days. By the time the enemy reach Amiens they will be starving, they'll have empty rifles and full hospital tents.' He drank the red wine and rose to his feet. 'Now I must get back to the school. General Bruce will arrive tomorrow morning and I want you, Colette, to be there.'

'I can't spy on the Germans from Aimee's school,' the woman laughed.

Captain Ellis put his hat back on his head. 'No but you can help me spy on the British. The Germans have spies too. And one of them is in our general's office, passing our secrets to the enemy. I want you to help me trap him.'

'How?' Colette Fletcher asked.

'Act as a cleaner for the old school. Then you can go everywhere. The spy is too careful to let me see him at work. But he won't pay any attention to a cleaner.'

'Or a girl,' Aimee said. 'I'm coming too, Maman. I'm going to be a White Lady like you. *Intus est hostis*,' she said.

'The enemy is within the gates.' Captain Ellis nodded. 'He is indeed. You are welcome to join us in the hunt for him.'

And that was how Aimee set off on the search for the most dangerous man in France.

22 March 1918: East of Peronne

Marius woke from a restless sleep with dreams of finding his wounded father on a battlefield, pouring the potion into his mouth and seeing him rise up as strong as ever. He shook his head. He knew it was just a dream and he remembered a poem from his school days...

'That no life lives for ever;
That dead men rise up never.'

He remembered where he was and looked up into the face of the fat baker who was grinning down at him. 'Well done, lad, well done.'

'Sorry? What?' he muttered as he rubbed at his tired eyes.

'Your magic drink. Look what it did for the little shoemaker.'

The skinny man who had seemed so sick the night before was looking as pale and grey as ever, but his eyes were clearer and his breathing was now easy. 'I thought I was finished,' he said. 'I was sure I'd wake up dead.'

The lorry had stopped at a camp of tents in a field that led down to the River Somme. There was bustle and the noise of lorries with groaning springs and coughing engines, the smell of petrol and horse sweat and the toilet trenches.

'Come on, lad, they need you over there,' the baker said. Marius clutched his backpack and let the large man lead him over to a long tent bearing a white circle with a red cross inside. The smell of blood hung heavy. 'Who's in charge?' the baker cried. A worried-looking man in a red-stained white coat glanced up from where he was kneeling beside a croaking soldier.

'What do you want?' he snapped. He pushed his spectacles back on his nose. His brown hair fell over his face, too long and neglected.

'This lad wants to join the hospital service, doctor. He has the most marvellous cure for the flu.'

The doctor snorted. 'We need nurses not miracle-workers. Here, lad, take your pack off, put a white coat on and help me with this new lot of wounded. Mostly shell and shot wounds from the battle for Peronne.'

The baker shrugged and walked back to the lorry waving. 'Good luck, lad.'

Marius found himself spending the rest of the day cutting off boots and uniforms so the doctors could see the wounds then changing the bandages that had been roughly tied on in battle. He pressed down on spouting wounds while the doctors sewed them shut and he helped when there were shattered arms and legs to be removed. There were lice to be dodged, which was tricky as some men were swarming with them.

And still lorries arrived with new batches of sick and dying. Some of the wounded stayed cheerful. 'We'll be in Peronne tomorrow,' a limping soldier told the tent and there was a weak cheer from those who had the strength left.

'We'll be in Amiens a week from now,' he went on.

Someone laughed and shouted, 'Not with these wounds, my friend. The war's over for me.'

'Where will I be on Tuesday?' the sour-faced doctor asked. 'It's my birthday. Will I get to spend it in Paris with the best French wines?'

The limping soldier seemed to take the question seriously. 'Paris in June, I'd say. But next Tuesday? Ah, next Tuesday I'd guess we'll be nice and comfy a dozen kilometres down the Somme... probably that nice little village by the river. We took it four years ago.'

'What's it called?' Marius asked, looking at the tattered map he pulled from his pocket.

'Bray, I think it's called,' the soldier told him. 'Bray-on-Somme.'

22 March 1918: Bray

As Aimee and her mother walked down to the school they struggled to get through the traffic. The sleepy village of Bray had become a whirlpool of war.

Motor-lorries and horse wagons of weapons were heading east to supply the men fighting the enemy who were driving forward. The precious heavy guns and tanks were being sent west to Amiens to save them from being captured. As before, when the two convoys met in Bray, they became tangled in the tiny, twisting lanes.

Angry drivers swore and struggled with sweating horses. Weary wounded men stumbled along at the edge of the ditches. Some had their eyes bandaged and rested a hand on the shoulder of the man in front.

'They've been blinded by German gas attacks,' Colette Fletcher explained. Aimee gave a small gasp and her mother said quickly, 'Most of them will see again, once the wet bandages are taken off.'

As they reached the corner of their lane a sergeant stood and sent the wounded up to their farm. The day before Captain Ellis had said, 'We need to use your barn as a hospital.'

Colette Fletcher had agreed at once. 'We won't be needing it for hay for a couple of months.'

The walking wounded were followed by ambulances carrying the men too sick to march. The crunching of the wheels on the rutted lane was echoed by the moans of the men inside the red-crossed wagons.

When they reached the school the cat had gone. There was as much turmoil in the old building as in the rest of the village. School desks were out in the schoolyard and heavy cabinets and office desks were being moved in. 'Waste of time,' a tired soldier grumbled. 'The enemy will be here in a couple of days and we'll have to move out again.'

'We've been sent to help with the cleaning,' Colette Fletcher said. That was the story they'd agreed with Captain Ellis.

'Report to Silver Hand,' the soldier told them.

'Who?'

'Sergeant Grimm. He has a metal hand. He's in charge of General Bruce's office.'

Mother and daughter entered the building and found the man easily. He was standing in the middle of the school hall bawling orders at soldiers who were scurrying around like beetles. 'Start with the classroom in the corner,' he snapped. 'That will be General Bruce's office.' Colette's eyes were fixed on his gleaming left hand of solid metal.

Sergeant Grimm raised his chin. 'I see you're wondering about my hand? Don't be afraid to ask. It's a war wound. I went into no man's land and saved my commander. He was shot in the leg and trapped in a shell-hole. The enemy tried to bring me down with two machine guns but I crawled on my belly with the bullets bouncing off my helmet. I saved his life.'

'And the hand was hit?' Colette Fletcher asked.

'Yes. I'd just got him back to the safety of our trenches – I was using my body to shield him – and one last bullet shattered my hand. As it happened the commander was from a rich family and wanted to reward me. He said I should have a new hand made of solid silver. If I ever fell on hard times, after the war, I could snap off a finger and sell it.'

37

'You're a hero,' Colette said. 'Did they give you a medal?'

'They offered me one but I told them no. I was only doing what any true British soldier would do. I was proud to serve my country. I don't need a medal.'

He turned on his heel and screamed at a small soldier struggling with a desk. 'Put your back into it, you miserable midget.'

Colette and Aimee slipped into the classroom and began work. 'Go into the wall cupboard and pack the schoolbooks in a box,' Colette said. 'I'll start polishing the desk for the general.'

Aimee nodded and entered the cool, dark cupboard in the wall. The shelves were stacked with worn and dusty books. She saw her favourite, Cicero, and began reading as she heard the door to the classroom swing open.

'Sergeant Grimm,' said a man's voice.

'Yes, General.'

'I need a word in private.'

'Yes, General.' Sergeant Grimm coughed. 'Excuse me, cleaner. Can you leave the room for a couple of minutes? Sorry to disturb your work.'

'Excellent work, by the way, Madame,' the general added.

'Thank you, sir, I'll start on the school hall,' Colette Fletcher said in a humble voice. She was playing a good game of being a spy. And she knew her daughter was quietly working in the cupboard. Listening. Whatever Colette missed, Aimee would hear. She remembered Captain Ellis's words in her home the day before: 'There is a spy in General Bruce's office. We have to find him.'

Aimee put the book down quietly and pressed herself into the shadows as near to the door as she could without being seen.

General Bruce rustled some papers. 'Before we do anything, Sergeant Grimm, I need you to make sure the secret papers you put in the safe back in Amiens are locked away here. Do we have a safe in this office yet?'

'Yes, sir, on the floor under the desk.'

'Good. Make sure they stay inside and always post a guard outside the door. They have a secret that can win us the war... so long as the enemy never gets to know about it.'

'You can trust me, sir.'

'Good work, Sergeant, now carry on...' the general said. Aimee heard the office door open then close as he left the room. Aimee wondered if she should step out of the cupboard now. But she heard a small bell ring and a click as Sergeant Grimm picked up the general's telephone and began to speak.

Aimee held her breath and strained her ears.

Chapter Two

'A traitor does not look like a traitor'

22 March 1918: Bray

'Hello, operator?' Sergeant Grimm said softly. 'Can you put me through to Sector Eight in Cléry?'

There was a long pause while the call was connected and the soldier appeared to be shuffling papers as he waited. Aimee didn't risk looking out. The air in the cupboard was filled with dust from the old books and she wanted to sniff but didn't dare.

'Hello?' Grimm said finally. 'Benedict? Yes, sorry I've been out of touch. It has been difficult to get to a phone. Do you have a pencil? This will have to be very quick.' The sergeant began to speak in a low voice as rapid as the jabber of a machine gun. 'This is a secret they'll pay us a fortune for. The British have a new sort of gas... No, our German friends can't keep it out with gas masks. It is sent over in shells and makes a smoke cloud. Gas masks are useless.'

Sergeant Grimm listened. Then he went on. 'It gives the soldiers pains in the mouth, nose, eyes and throat, and pains in the chest. They struggle to breathe then they start throwing up. That's right. They can't fight on like that. But it's not like the gases we use now. It wears off and it doesn't kill the enemy. The British can take prisoners but don't have to waste time treating them in hospitals.'

He listened again. 'If our German friends get the formula for this secret gas before the British start to use it then they may be able to make new gas masks that can keep it out... or even make the gas themselves and use it against the Brits. They will give us our weight in gold for this. So, are you ready?'

There was a rustling of papers again and Aimee knew she had discovered the traitor. She also knew that Sergeant Grimm might kill to keep his treason secret. If she walked into the room she could save the British and French so much trouble. And she also might die. Grimm was speaking quickly again. 'They call it diphenylamine chlorarsine. I'll spell it for you then give you the formula for how to make it.'

Sergeant Grimm gave his partner the details. Then he explained how it would be used. 'The men in the trenches will put canisters of this DM gas on the edge of their own trenches. They'll light a fuse and the wind will carry the cloud across no man's land. When the Germans are coughing and vomiting the British will attack. They'll give their own men special gas masks so they don't suffer.'

Aimee knew she should have stopped him. She couldn't decide... until the dust decided for her. She sneezed. The man with the silver hand muttered something in German and put down the telephone. Aimee made herself busy with packing the books into a box. Sergeant Grimm's shadow turned the dark room into a tomb. He filled the dusty air with the scent of tobacco and sweat. She looked up at him and gave a warm smile. '*Bonjour, Monsieur*,' she said.

'Do you speak English, girl?' the man asked and the fingers on his good hand rippled like a pianist's. Aimee shivered.

'*Pardon*?' she said.

Grimm smiled and said, 'That's good. If you spoke English I'd have to kill you.' The words were spoken in a soft and friendly voice.

'*Pardon*?'

'Get out.'

'*Pardon*?'

He waved his silver hand at the door. Aimee pointed at the books and made a mime of packing them. The man shook his head and pointed at the door from the cupboard. She shrugged and walked past him into the office and towards the door into the hall. Silver Hand spoke soft as a butterfly's wing. 'You dropped some paper,' he said in English.

Aimee almost stopped and turned to look for it. She remembered she wasn't supposed to understand English and carried on. But that half stop was enough. Silver Hand knew. And Aimee knew he meant what he said. To keep his deadly secret safe he would have to kill her. And kill her soon.

23 March 1918: Peronne

The doctor with the spectacles and the worried face was called Weger. Marius soon learned that the doctor's miserable appearance hid a sharp mind that loved to joke. The boy followed him through the hospital tents, weary as a fox at the end of a hunt. Doctor Weger never seemed to get tired. At night they moved, always west, chasing the setting sun.

'I sleep as we travel,' the doctor said.

Marius just nodded wearily and dozed. He woke to find the army had moved forward ten kilometres in the last day. 'We are driving them to the sea,' a wounded soldier with a torn shoulder said. 'I saw the British running away from us. Running. The war will be over in a week.'

But by the end of the day the soldier was grumbling about his hunger. 'The supply wagons can't keep up with us,' Doctor Weger told him. 'The British are running too fast.'

The wounded soldier spat on the ground. 'The generals don't care about our bellies.'

The doctor pushed his spectacles back on to his nose. 'And the medicines we need can't keep up with us either,' he told the soldier. 'We have so many fever cases. More men are falling sick with flu than from bullets.'

'I have a cure for the fever,' Marius said quietly. 'My grandmother taught me.'

The doctor looked at him. 'Witchcraft was it? Eye of newt and toe of frog stuff?'

'No, she made it from the bark of a willow tree.'

The doctor nodded slowly. 'Yes. Willow tree bark. Our German chemists have been making it for twenty years now. They call it Aspirin. We don't have any.'

'But we're near the River Somme,' Marius said. 'I've seen willow trees on the banks. I can make willow tea from the bark.'

Again Doctor Weger nodded. 'The men in the fever tent are dying. We have nothing to lose, young man. I'll send a couple of fit men to help you collect the bark. But hurry. We'll be moving on again tonight.'

And so Marius's new life began. Each day he gathered the willow bark and stewed it to make his fever cure. Some men were cured and some were as ill as ever. But Marius had moved on ever westwards before he saw them killed or cured.

The soldiers who came to the hospital tents were exhausted now. They weren't singing songs about driving the British back any longer. They were complaining of tiredness and hunger and always that fever, which was striking down their friends. Every night they moved west. Every night they moved less than the night before.

As the sun rose on Tuesday 26th March Doctor Weger took Marius with him through the woods so they could be closer to the fighting than the boy had ever been. They stood at the edge of the trees, high on a ridge above the River Somme, and looked down on the war below.

The air was filled with sounds like whistles or screams. Fountains of earth leaped towards the sky as shells exploded overhead like inky-black flowers. The ground shook and between the explosions there was the droning of aeroplanes battling across the morning sky. White clouds of steam hurried across the valley. Great oak trees lay shattered where the armies had battled through.

The doctor raised an arm and pointed to the plain below them. 'That's Bray, the railhead for the British. If we capture that we can stay a while and set up a proper hospital.'

'We aren't going to follow our army to the sea? Watch them drive the British to their ships?' Marius asked.

The doctor shook his head. 'No. We'll have to stop soon. We're like a steam engine and our fires are burning low. Bray will be a good place to rest.'

26 March 1918: Bray

Aimee had spent four days and nights in fear. When Sergeant Grimm the traitor followed her from the classroom into the school hall he laid his cold silver hand on her shoulder. 'Don't be afraid, little girl. So long as you keep your mouth shut you will come to no harm.'

She stared up into his dark hawk eyes that were as hot as his hand was cold. 'Of course,' he went on quietly, 'if you tell anyone what you just heard then I will know. And children have accidents in days of war. Crushed by a tank. Trampled by a horse. Blown apart by a hand grenade that someone carelessly dropped. We don't want that happening to you, do we?'

Before Aimee could answer, the door from the corridor opened and Captain Ellis strode in. He spoke in French. 'Ah, Aimee, your mother's looking for you. She has a broomstick she wants you to deliver.'

Aimee nodded and fled from under the icy silver hand. She spent three days running to villages nearby, delivering broomsticks and beans for the White Lady. When the Germans arrived then the spies would be ready to start sending messages to their British friends.

British soldiers marched past her, heading west, torn and bandaged from their fighting. Now their songs were gloomier.

'Take me back to dear old Blighty!
Put me on the train for London town!

Take me over there,
Drop me anywhere,
Birmingham, Leeds or Manchester, well,
I don't care!'

Aimee's father had told her 'Blighty' was the soldiers' name for Britain. Their singing was sweet but their eyes were dead in their grey faces, their boots dusty, and their feet dragged. They'd had enough of war. They just wanted to go home. To anywhere.

Every time Aimee returned to Bray from the villages the thunder of the guns seemed closer. The streets were more crowded with the fleeing British. Their barn was full of wounded men and the sky was forever clouded with sooty smoke from the trains at the railhead, taking men away and bringing in new bullets and bombs to fight the battle. A battle they knew was lost.

When she went to meet her mother in the school the man with the silver hand seemed to be watching her from every shadow. A small smile played on his thin, cruel lips. The lips seemed to say, 'We have a secret. Keep it secret.'

On Tuesday 26th March a huge lorry pulled into the drive of Mrs Fletcher's farm. It carried a folded package as dull as lead. Other lorries brought cables and machines and Aimee watched as a motor pump blew into the package and turned it into a great grey balloon, the shape of a cigar and as large as the barn.

Men hurried to fasten cables to it as a breeze caught the balloon and lifted it a little. 'I've never seen one close up,' Colette told her daughter. 'I guess they are going to fly into the air to look down on the enemy... see how close they are and what they're doing.'

'We are,' Captain Ellis said. He'd been standing behind them watching the forty soldiers prepare for the flight. 'And I'm the one who gets the lucky job of going up with the camera.'

'I thought the aeroplanes took pictures?' Mrs Fletcher said.

Captain Ellis shrugged. 'They do... but the Germans have aircraft too and they try to shoot ours down. It's dangerous. They have a new airfield beside the Somme. Their best fighter pilots are all there. They are blowing us out of the sky.'

Aimee laughed. 'But the balloon's dangerous too. The enemy can shoot down balloons.'

The captain shook his head. 'Not if we haul it down as soon as we have the photos. I've never known the Germans shoot down a single balloon.' He led the way to a larger wicker basket that hung below the whale-belly balloon. He lifted the girl into the basket. 'There are two ropes under the gas bag – pull this one and you float down slowly. But pull this one with the red ribbon round it and you drop very quickly. Far too quickly for an enemy fighter to catch you in the air. Red for danger.'

'Would you like to go up with the captain, Aimee?' her mother asked. 'See what it's like to fly?'

Aimee's eyes sparkled. 'More than anything,' she beamed.

The young soldier climbed into the basket and began to give orders to the ground crew to let them float upwards. As the last rope was ready for untying there came a cry: 'Stop! Captain Ellis.'

Aimee looked over the edge of the basket and saw Sergeant Grimm waving a sheet of paper in his good hand. He panted as if he'd run from the school. 'Sorry, sir, General Bruce needs you in the office. It's urgent.'

Captain Ellis frowned. 'So is this flight. We need the photos as soon as possible so we can see where to fire our guns.'

'Not a problem,' the sergeant said. 'I can do that. Done it a dozen times.'

And, before Aimee could find the words to escape, Captain Ellis had jumped out and Silver Hand was in the basket beside her. This time his grin was as wide as the Somme. 'Hello, my little friend. I'm going to enjoy this trip.' He turned to the men on the ground. 'Cast off,' he ordered and Aimee felt the balloon leap upwards with a jerk that sent her stomach into her mouth.

The spring sunshine was hidden by the great grey monster over their heads and the breeze felt cold. Or maybe it was Aimee's fear. Soon they were higher than the tops of the spindly trees and sending startled birds squawking away. The people below were shrinking and she saw her mother wave happily. Colette Fletcher didn't know. Aimee had been too afraid of the threat from the man with the silver hand to say anything. And now it was too late.

The black road was a ribbon spattered with the khaki and brown of lorries and marching men. The Somme looked peaceful and shiny green while the railway yards hid under a haze of smoke.

To the east Aimee could see the flashes of the enemy guns pouring shells down on the ground, closer and closer to Bray. Her farm looked small enough to be a doll's house and the animals were dots in the smooth green of the fields.

Tears filled her eyes and blurred the scene. It was beautiful. It was the last thing she'd ever see, she knew.

Aimee was expecting the grip of Sergeant Grimm's hand on her smock but it still made her sick when she felt it.

'So sad,' Silver Hand said. 'A girl goes in an air balloon for the first time. She panics and runs around and falls out.'

The strong right hand lifted her so she was half out of the basket. She couldn't find the breath to cry.

'Goodbye, Aimee,' said Silver Hand.

26 March 1918: East of Bray

Doctor Weger and Marius looked down from the ridge on to the town of Bray. 'The Romans used to fight on elephants,' Marius said.

The doctor gave a sudden laugh. 'What?'

'I didn't know the British still used them,' the boy said and pointed to a field on the edge of the town. 'Well, it looks like an elephant to me.'

The doctor moved his head and went stiff. 'It's a balloon. A hundred times more deadly than an elephant,' he croaked.

'A balloon can't hurt you,' Marius argued.

Doctor Weger took a deep breath and spoke quickly. 'It will rise in the air with at least one man in a basket below. He will take pictures of this wood. The pictures will show where our big guns are. The British will pour shells down on our gunners. They could kill fifty of our men and wreck a dozen guns.

Marius shivered and watched as the grey monster swelled. 'What can we do?'

'Shoot it down.'

'I haven't got a gun,' the boy said.

'I mean send a message to the aerodrome and get a fighter plane to shoot it down.' The doctor turned to the boy and gripped his shoulders. 'The nearest aerodrome is just off the Peronne road. A farmer's field turned into an airstrip. You can run there faster than I could.'

'How far?'

'Five kilometres.'

'I can run that in twenty minutes,' Marius said.

'It will take that long to get the balloon in position. You might just get there in time. Now go.'

Marius turned back on to the track through the wood. He leaped over roots and clambered over trunks of trees that had been shattered by shells. He tripped on a broken branch from time to time, rolled and picked himself up, always moving forward.

At the far side of the trees he saw a field sloping down to the road. It was crowded with trucks but they would be no use to him. They were all moving westwards towards Bray. His boots clattered on the road and he had to weave around the groaning lorries. His lungs started to burn and his legs grew weak from the lack of good food. He pictured

British shells landing among his comrades and found new strength.

His boots were heavy as houses. He paused, took them off and threw them over his shoulder. Marius sprinted on. The road sloped downwards towards the river. At last he saw the aeroplanes on the grass and the pilots sitting outside their tents while mechanics worked on the planes, filling them with fuel and loading the guns.

The grass was soft under his feet. A guard inside the gate tried to stop him. Marius gasped, 'Urgent message,' and raced across the airfield.

One of the pilots looked up from a game of cards and his pale thin lips twisted into a smile. 'What's the hurry, soldier?'

Marius's lungs ached and his mouth was so dry his voice was a crow croak. 'There's a balloon going up... farm field near Bray...'

The pilot jumped to his feet. 'Then we'll have to shoot it down,' he laughed. He strode across to the rows of planes. Some were painted in camouflage green but others – the fast fighters – were painted bright colours as if to say: 'Come and shoot me if you dare.'

The pilot walked towards a bright red plane with three wings. 'Is number 477 ready to fly?' he barked at a grease-covered mechanic.

'Five minutes, Baron,' the man replied. 'We're changing the oil and...'

'In five minutes a hundred men could be dead.' He looked around the airfield. 'What is ready to go *now*?'

'The Albatross J2, Baron.'

The pilot was pulling on a leather coat and flying helmet as he marched across to one of the dull planes with two wings and two seats. He looked over his shoulder at Marius and called, 'The British fighters will be ready to defend the balloon. I can't fight them in this bus. I need a gunner in the rear seat. You can be my gunner and show me where you saw that balloon.'

Marius hardly had time to gather his breath. He ran after the pilot as mechanics scurried around to make the plane ready for take-off. 'I don't think I can fire a machine gun.'

'Of course you can. Every soldier learns it in basic training.'

Marius almost blurted that he had done no basic training. He had no right to be there. But the pilot – the Baron – was already climbing on to the wing of the plane. 'You know the plan,' he called to the other pilots who were heading for the small planes with three wings. They answered with salutes. He then turned to the boy. 'Where are we going?' he asked.

'Five kilometres north-west of here. Near the town of Bray.'

'I know it,' the pilot said as he hauled himself into the cockpit and a mechanic helped Marius into the seat behind the pilot. The pilot pressed switches and gave a thumbs-up sign to one of the ground crew who swung the propeller round.

The engine rasped, sputtered and sparked into life. Marius struggled back into his boots as the plane turned round and began to race and bump over the grassy field. The wooden frame creaked and groaned then the rattling of the wheels suddenly stopped as it lifted into the air.

The wind took the breath out of Marius's body and the speed pressed him back in his seat. Fumes of petrol and castor oil filled his nose while the wind sang through the wires that held the plane together.

As they soared towards the clouds the pilot levelled off and circled. Marius saw the balloon at the same time as the man in front of him. From the skies it appeared a much smaller elephant than it had looked from the woods and Marius wondered how they could hit such a tiny target.

The pilot nudged the controls and the plane began a flat run towards it a kilometre away. Suddenly brown smoke mushrooms appeared in the air beside them and splinters of shell spattered against the plane – the British gunners on the ground were ready for this sort of attack and were firing at them. The pilot held steady and the balloon began to loom larger. Marius strained forward and saw two pale faces staring at him from the basket.

One was a man in British army uniform. But the other seemed to be a girl in a smock dress and the man was lifting her above the side of the basket. 'It's a girl,' Marius screamed. 'Don't shoot.'

Through the roar of the wind and the engine the pilot didn't seem to hear. Marius reached forward and slapped the man hard on the shoulder just as he took one hand off the controls to press the trigger on the machine gun facing forward.

The plane lurched, the bullets sprayed wide of the grey monster. Hot gusts of air from the gun blew back in Marius's face. The pilot turned and looked back angrily. 'You made me miss.'

'But it's a girl in there,' Marius cried.

'One girl or dozens of our gunners,' the man shouted in reply. 'Sit down. I'm going in for a second pass.'

The plane wheeled through the sky and turned back towards its helpless target. The faces of the man and girl had vanished.

This time he wouldn't miss.

26 March 1918: East of Bray

As Silver Hand held the girl over the side of basket he felt the balloon jerk. The ground crew had seen the German plane before Sergeant Grimm or Aimee had.

'Albatross J2 from the east,' an officer barked. 'Height one thousand feet. Prepare to fire anti-aircraft guns... and get the balloon down as fast as you can.'

'It won't be fast enough, Captain,' a soldier said as he put the cable motor into reverse and started to wind in the cable.

He was right. It was slow, too slow. Still, the sharp downward tug of the cables sent Silver Hand falling backwards into the basket and Aimee fell alongside him. They struggled to their feet and looked at the nose of the aircraft whirring towards them. They looked down the barrels of two machine guns.

The plane swerved a little as the guns spat their fire and the ripple of bullets missed. In a moment the plane had rolled on its side and was turning for a second attack. Aimee watched, helpless, as the enemy came back. The pilot in goggles seemed to be arguing with a small soldier in the back seat whose pale face looked afraid.

Anti-aircraft shells were exploding around the plane as the men on the ground tried to track it and shoot it down. But it was moving too fast.

'Where are those fighter planes we were promised? The Sopwith Camels?' the British officer groaned.

Sergeant Grimm had sunk into the furthest corner of the basket and had wrapped his knees in his arms, as if he could protect himself from the bullets that way. He was moaning, 'Dear God, please save me. Save me.'

The German pilot had the balloon lined up in his sights now and was heading straight towards Aimee, half a kilometre away.

As Aimee looked back at Sergeant Grimm, who had his eyes closed and seemed to be praying, a rope caught her face. The rope had a red ribbon wrapped around it and she remembered. She pulled hard on the rope. There was a pause then the balloon valve opened and they began to drop like an eagle on a mouse below.

The enemy pilot who had fired his guns was a hundred metres from them when he opened fire again. But he found himself shooting at where the falling balloon had been. He pulled the control stick and soared upwards as the ground guns poured their shattering shells towards him. He weaved across the sky to put them off and made his way back east towards his airfield.

A gunner in the ground crew looked to the west and cried, 'British fighter planes on their way. Stop firing.'

From the west a flight of three planes roared across the River Somme. Red, white and blue roundels were painted on the stubby wings. 'Sopwith Camels.' A soldier nodded. 'They'll get him. German swine.'

The gunners cheered but the rest of the crew were hurrying across to where the basket had landed. Aimee and Sergeant Grimm had hit the ground fast and were thrown out on to the soft ploughed field. Aimee lay there, shaken, while the sergeant wailed, 'I've lost my hand. The strap's snapped. Help me find my hand. It's solid silver, you know.' Men began to search the field and a soldier quickly found it, shining in the dark ploughed earth.

Aimee picked herself up. She was shaking and aching. Once she was sure she had no broken bones she ran across the field to the farmhouse and crashed through the kitchen door.

'Aimee,' her mother cried. 'You're a mess. Covered in dirt – pigtails coming loose. What have you been up to?'

The girl began to tell her story and Mrs Fletcher scowled. 'I should never have let you go up. I put your life in danger,'

'You're one of the White Lady spies, Maman. Your life will be in danger too when the Germans get here. They're just on the other side of the woods. I saw them.'

'It's not the same,' her mother said.

Aimee took a deep breath and blurted, 'He tried to kill me.'

'Of course he did. That's the German pilot's job.'

'Not the pilot. Sergeant Grimm. He tried to throw me out of the balloon basket. If the German pilot hadn't turned up and started shooting, he would have done.'

Mrs Fletcher turned pale. 'Why would Sergeant Grimm want to do that?'

Aimee told her about the traitor's telephone call to Benedict. 'Why didn't you tell me this before?' Mrs Fletcher asked in a low voice.

'He said he'd kill me if I told anyone,' Aimee replied.

Her mother spread her hands. 'He tried to kill you anyway. It's the only way he'll be sure you won't talk.'

'I know,' Aimee whispered. 'What can I do?'

Mrs Fletcher picked up a shawl and threw it across her shoulders. 'Captain Ellis is looking for a spy. Now I can tell him who it is. You stay here and feed the lambs for me.'

She found Captain Ellis in the old school, packing away the office they'd set up just a few days before. In the bustle of the hurrying men he listened. 'Aimee's word is not enough. No one else heard the phone call. But we can watch Silver Hand now. Even set a trap for him. Though it will have to wait. The Germans will be here tomorrow. If we remain in Bray they'll destroy it with their guns. We need to get back to Amiens.'

'I'll stay here and keep spying for you.'

'You're a brave woman, Mrs Fletcher.'

Colette pretended to pick something off the floor to hide her blushes. 'I have Aimee to help me. Together we'll make life hard for the Germans. Goodbye for now. I'll see you when you return,' she said with a faint smile.

Captain Ellis nodded. 'We will be back.'

But it would take longer than he thought.

26 March 1918: East of Bray

Marius watched in horror as three British fighter planes began to close in on the Baron's Albatross. His pilot shouted, 'Shoot at them.'

The boy looked down the barrel of the machine gun, lined up one of the Camels and pulled the trigger. 'It's not working,' he cried.

The Baron steadied the plane, stood up in his seat and turned around. He pulled a small lever on the side of the gun. 'Safety catch off first, idiot.' He threw himself back into his seat and dived towards the River Somme, weaving to throw the enemy off his tail.

A Camel followed every move and was just fifty metres behind Marius now. The boy pulled the trigger and the gun crashed into life. Bullets spewed wide of the Camel but the enemy pilot panicked and threw his plane out of the way.

Then the Baron began firing his own gun that pointed forward as a second Camel attacked from in front of the Albatross. The British pilot fired too. Marius watched as bullets stitched a line of holes through the wings to his right and the tail-plane behind him. The next time the stitching could be through him.

Then he saw their airfield ahead where pilots and crew were running around like ants. He felt like cheering. They were almost safe. The German planes had large white patches with black crosses on their colourful wings. The Baron flew low over the field then soared upwards again.

'Why aren't we landing?' the boy wailed.

The pilot shouted over his shoulder, 'Because if we land they will shoot us like ducks on a pond.' He saw another Camel appear over the head of Marius and swerved. 'Keep firing.'

Again the wild stream of lead sent the enemy diving away for safety.

The Baron looked around again. 'Now we are not ducks on a pond. We are the decoy duck. While the British are shooting at our poor helpless little plane the rest of my squadron are climbing in the clouds like falcons waiting to swoop.'

There was a distant pattering rattle of machine guns and the Baron grinned. 'And here they come,' he said.

Marius swung round in his seat to see six coloured triplanes dive down on to the surprised Camels. They were a rainbow of death. They swooped and twisted like the falcons the Baron had promised. Marius watched, mouth open, and almost felt sorry for the British pilots.

The Camels turned towards the river and headed back west with the triplane hornets stinging them with bullets. One Camel was on fire, its engine spilling black plumes behind it, then it disappeared from his sight as the Baron brought their two-seater in to land gently on the grass and coast towards the village of tents on the edge of the airfield.

The engine stopped and steamed and crackled. The pilot climbed down and waited for Marius to join him on the ground, legs shaking and heart drumming. Mechanics ran towards the plane to lift the damaged tail-plane and pull it away to be repaired.

A tall man in a cap with a ghost-gaunt face strolled across. 'Well done, Manfred. Did we get the balloon?'

'No. This soldier spoiled my aim. The balloon went down but I don't think I hit it.'

'It didn't have time to take pictures though?'

'No, Commandant, but it will live to fly another day.' He looked across the airfield towards the red triplane. 'I'm off to hunt British turkeys, but first I will shoot this boy. Stand him in the middle of the field and I will use him as a target to warm up my guns.'

'Manfred,' the thin officer moaned. 'You know you can't do that.'

'I am Manfred von Richthofen, Germany's greatest hero of the skies. No one will dare to punish me.'

He strutted away to the red plane, which was ready to fly. 'I've heard of him,' Marius said. 'The Red Baron, they call him. He really is our greatest hero. Will he shoot me?'

'Only if you run.' The pale officer sighed. 'Stand in the middle of the field. He will fly towards you. Look him in the eye and he will admire your courage. Turn and run and he may do something nasty.'

Minutes later the boy stood wearily in the middle of the grass field that the pilots were using as an airfield today. Every few days they moved forward as their army advanced. A cool wind blew across the Somme and he shivered. He forced himself to stand as straight and tall as he could.

The red plane circled and droned then came low towards him, almost the height of Marius's head. The boy's eyes were filled with tears. He looked straight into the goggles of the Red Baron, raised an arm and saluted. Manfred Von Richthofen raised a quick hand in reply as the plane roared over Marius and almost blew him down.

The boy swallowed hard and walked slowly from the airfield towards the army hospital. The thin officer called, 'Boy!'

Marius turned. 'Well done,' the man grinned.

Chapter Three

'The life given us, by nature is short'

27 March 1918: Bray

Smoke hung grey over Bray like a shroud over a coffin. The British had given up and run west towards Amiens the evening before. They choked the roads with gun-carriages and men, with ambulances and lorries full of weapons, tools and barbed wire, food supplies and tanks.

They couldn't carry everything to safety. They burned their mounds of horse food before they left the town so the weary German horses couldn't eat it when they arrived. Anything that could be useful to the enemy was wrecked. Even the straw in the hospital beds at the Fletchers' barn was scattered over the floor.

The last trains pulled out of Bray station heading for safety in Amiens and gangs of British and French took iron bars to wreck the signals and the points.

The German army crept into the smoky town next morning, afraid of a trap, but they found it empty of enemy soldiers.

When they were sure it was clear they roared in with their motor-lorries and carts. Their drums rumbled and growled. The French people who'd stayed in Bray watched them silently. The British had been their allies. The Germans were their invaders – for the second time in four years.

A shambling band played a marching tune that the Bray folk knew was called 'The Glory of Germany'. It had been written in 1871 after the Germans defeated them in the last war between the two nations. It grated on the French ears and stabbed at the French hearts.

A German colonel with medal ribbons climbed on to the steps of the Town Hall and spoke to the people, who gathered round like sullen, sulking children. He spoke in good, clear French. 'We do not wish to harm anyone in Bray. Our war is against your soldiers and the British.'

'And the Americans,' a greengrocer muttered. 'Wait till they get here.'

If the colonel heard him he gave no sign but went on. 'We need every spare room that you have to shelter our soldiers. Your houses will be inspected and you will take as many men as you can fit in.' He paused and looked around with a small smile as if to say 'sorry'. 'We do not *want* to harm you but if anyone tries to hurt or obstruct us then they will be taken out and shot. Do I make myself clear?'

No one answered. He gave a tiny shrug and strode away towards the school. The Bray people shuffled off to suffer their visitors.

At the school door Master DuPont stood while the cat wrapped itself around his legs, weaving in and out but never taking its amber eyes off the German colonel coming up the path.

'Good day, Colonel,' the teacher said. 'I hope you have come to tell me I can open the school again. There are still a few children left in Bray.'

'I have come to take over your school for my offices,' the German officer said.

Master DuPont gave a small smile then let it slide away as secretly as it had come. 'Then allow me to help you.'

'Sensible man,' the colonel said.

'The British left yesterday...'

'They ran away,' the colonel sneered.

Master DuPont bowed his head. 'As you say, sir. But they left the school in a terrible mess. Perhaps I can let you have my cleaner to help you keep the place tidy. She is called Madame Fletcher.'

'Fletcher? An English name?'

'Indeed. Her husband was English. Now she has a small farm on the edge of town. Should I go and ask her to clean for you?'

'Yes. Hurry.'

Master DuPont walked quickly away with that secret smile – the smile of a spy – still on his face. He hadn't thought it would be so easy to get a White Lady into the German headquarters. The cat looked at the German officer's dusty boots and hissed.

A German sergeant arrived at Colette Fletcher's farm before the teacher. He explained in stumbling

French that the house would be filled with soldiers who would sleep on mattresses in the farmhouse attic and cellar.

'Not the barn?' Colette Fletcher asked.

'We need that for a hospital,' the sergeant told her. He looked over his shoulder to where a thin man in spectacles walked up the lane with a boy hurrying beside him. 'Here is Doctor Weger now.'

Aimee watched the boy. She was surprised. Were the Germans so short of men they had to call on boys that young to fight? His boots were worn and his uniform shabby. He looked so twig-thin he would snap in a strong wind.

For a moment she almost felt sorry for the boy. Then she shook her head and muttered, 'He's German, so I hate him.'

As Mrs Fletcher took the doctor across the yard to inspect the barn the boy looked shyly across at Aimee. '*Ich bin Marius*,' he said.

Aimee shrugged. 'Don't speak German,' she said sourly. 'Only French, and English... and Latin.'

The boy's eyes lit up in his small face. He spoke in Latin. 'I loved Latin at school. I can speak to you in Latin.'

Aimee pinched her mouth tight and hissed through her teeth, 'Why would I want to speak to you?' then closed the farmhouse door.

April 1918: Bray

The days passed in a blur of danger and weariness. Aimee's mother sent her on trips with broomstick messages to villages in the west. The German guards took little notice of a girl and never stopped her.

Mrs Fletcher groaned one evening as she sat with her daughter in the kitchen, sipping wine by the light of a smoky oil lamp. 'We can count the soldiers and guns and tell the British how strong the Germans are in these parts. But I could tell them so much more if I only spoke German. There are all sorts of messages lying around the old school when I'm cleaning. I just don't know which ones are important. It would be sad if I stole a cook's order for bacon, only to get caught and shot.'

'Don't talk about getting shot,' Aimee whispered. They both spoke softly though there was no one to listen and the sound of lorries rumbling up the lane to the hospital barn went on most of the night.

Mrs Fletcher looked up as another rolled past. 'They move the wounded back to Germany by night. They don't want the German people to see how many of their men have been broken.'

'But the Germans are winning,' Aimee argued. 'They will be halfway to the Atlantic by now.'

'No, they were stopped a week ago before they even got to Amiens,' Mrs Fletcher said. 'Their army moved forward too quickly. The food and the fuel, the aeroplanes and the guns, just couldn't keep up.'

She paused as they heard a sound somewhere between a whistle and a scream. There was a flash of light followed by a boom. A shell exploded near the railhead as the British tried to destroy the enemy trains. 'In 1914 – the last time the Germans were here – the British aimed at the railhead but managed to drop shells on the town. Let's hope they are more careful this time.'

One lorry went past with a clanking sound as its wheels crushed the stones in the lane to powder. 'Hear that?' said Aimee's mother. 'Some German lorries are without tyres because they don't have enough rubber. They are running out of everything.'

The lorries rumbled on through the night. Aimee tried to sleep but the soldiers who were staying in the attic and cellar of the farmhouse scraped and clumped their boots on stairs and floors, shouted and cursed one another as they returned for a rest. Aimee was pleased she didn't understand their swearing.

The next morning it was drizzling with rain and the fields were turning muddy.

Master DuPont arrived with news. 'A British shell missed the railhead and destroyed a cottage. Old Madame Leclerc was killed. The German soldiers cleared the rubble but they'll leave the burial to our priest, Father Gaston.'

Aimee headed through the woods towards the river to find some acorns for the next message. Each acorn in the broomstick stood for a German tank. They had very few tanks – and they were snail-slow and broke down often – but the British wanted to know what their soldiers would face.

There was a soft chopping coming from further down the path towards the River Somme. Aimee walked softly down the damp path to spy on the enemy. A soldier in a uniform the colour of wood-smoke was cutting into a willow tree and peeling off the bark. He placed the strips carefully into a rotting leather bucket. As he turned the soldier looked up. It was the boy who'd been helping the German doctor. What did he call himself? Marius, was it?

The soldier gave a shy smile. 'Why are you killing that tree?' Aimee spat at him. He looked confused. She repeated it in Latin and the cloud cleared from the boy's face.

'I am making a drug to cure our sick men. They have flu. The sickness is killing more of our men than British guns.'

'The war will end quicker then,' the girl replied coldly.

Marius shrugged. 'It cannot go on much longer. Back in Germany the people are starving – that's why I joined the army. The British battleships are stopping our food ships from getting through. I left home so there was one less mouth for my mother to feed.'

'What about your father?'

'Missing after the battle at Verdun,' the boy said quietly. 'We hope he's a prisoner.'

'You're saying you left home to eat, not to kill?' she asked. It explained why he was so pale and thin.

'I left to help with the sick. I can't even fire a gun. I haven't been trained.'

'If you're all so hungry why don't you just go home and leave us in peace?' Aimee asked more gently.

'A lot of our soldiers are deserting because they know we are losing. I took this uniform from a soldier who'd run away from the fighting. The men are tired and hungry and this sickness is the last dagger in our hearts.'

'Then why doesn't King Wilhelm give up?'

The boy shook his head. 'He isn't hungry. He doesn't see the people that rebel on the streets of our cities back home. He doesn't see the sick men that I see.' The boy turned his wide eyes on Aimee. 'I know we Germans are your enemy. But we are just ordinary people – like you. We fight because that's what we have to do to live.'

Aimee narrowed her eyes. She saw a chance to spy for the White Lady. Her voice softened as if she felt sorry for the boy. 'Show me these sick men, Marius. Maybe I could help.'

'You would?'

Aimee nodded slowly. 'As you say, these are ordinary men – like my father. If I help to care for German husbands and fathers maybe a young German will care for my father if he's ever wounded or captured.'

They finished filling the bucket with the willow bark and turned back through the cool wood, walking through jagged stumps of trees where stray shells had snapped them.

'Do we have a truce?' Marius asked.

The girl thought for a moment. 'We can make peace for a little while.'

The boy muttered something in German. 'What was that?' Aimee asked.

'There is an English writer called William Shakespeare. We love to study him in German schools.'

'I've heard of him.'

'He said something about peace. He called it the silver hand of peace.'

Aimee shuddered and almost stumbled. The Silver Hand she knew would not bring peace to her if he ever returned.

April 1918: Bray

The first thing Aimee noticed as she entered her barn was the smell of sickness. Men lay in crowded rows, some talking to their neighbours, some moaning or breathing with grating breaths, some silent as the rain clouds outside.

Doctor Weger was moving between the mattresses on the floor giving medicine to some men and water to others. He gave a nod to Marius as the boy walked in, then looked at Aimee. 'The farm girl. Can I help you?' he asked in bad French.

Marius explained. 'She has come to help us.'

The doctor nodded. 'We have so few nurses that any help is welcome. Tell me, girl, have you ever had the flu?'

Aimee replied, 'Yes. At Christmas. I was sick for a week.'

'That is good. You will not catch it again, I think. You are well fed with your farm eggs and bread and milk. These soldiers are half starved. That makes them fall like corn when the Grim Reaper strikes.'

Marius hurried off with his bucket of willow bark to make more medicine. 'I hope Marius will not catch it. I need him,' the doctor said.

'It's just as well the British don't know how weak these men are,' Aimee said.

Doctor Weger sighed. 'If they did they would walk into Bray and take the town back with hardly a shot.'

The girl struggled to hide her smile. 'The British will know before the day is out,' she murmured.

'What was that?'

'I said, "how can I help you out?"' Marius helped her say it in German.

'It's a disgusting job but the toilet buckets need to be emptied into the trench at the back of the barn. Then some of the wounded men need their bandages changed. The ones who are strong enough will be sent back to Germany tonight. There's so much to do.' The doctor sighed.

Aimee worked for an hour then helped serve the men with tinned stew the British had left behind. 'It is worth falling sick to get this food,' Marius said as he helped spoon the rich gravy into bowls and carried them to the men who were well enough to eat. 'Most of us have not seen food like this for months. A few months ago we went through what we called the Turnip Winter because it seemed that was all we had to eat. We drank coffee made from acorns, the soldiers smoked tobacco made from beech-tree leaves, bakers stuffed our bread with sawdust, and butchers made sausages from horseflesh or rabbits. That's why I left home.'

Aimee said, 'Your soldiers get all the best food?'

'Yes.' Marius groaned as he stirred his stew. 'They eat quite well, but not as well as the French and the British. It hurts us to know our enemy eats like this every day. They even have jam for their bread.'

As the walking wounded helped clear away the meal, Aimee asked if she could run across to see her mother. Colette Fletcher was cleaning the stables when her daughter ran in with news of the German weakness.

'Shall I take a message to Cerisy so the White Lady spy there can pass it on to the British?' Aimee asked. 'We daren't use the radio in the barn.'

'No need. We have a new messenger in Bray. He walks there every day. He says he needs the exercise for his old legs now the school has been closed.'

'Master DuPont? Part of the White Lady spy web?' Aimee laughed. The thought of the old teacher being a secret agent was funny.

'He fought in the last war against the Germans back in 1871 and has been part of the White Lady since it was set up in this war. Now he's not busy at the school, he will be thrilled to carry messages. Get back to the barn. Find out more. Question the sick.'

'They're German. I can't talk to them.'

Colette slapped the side of her head. 'Of course. What was I thinking? But get what you can from the boy and the doctor.'

Aimee ran off as if there were springs in her boots. She was helping her country to win the war.

April 1918: Amiens

The message reached Amiens a day later. Captain Ellis took it to General Bruce. 'We could walk into Bray and take the town back with hardly a shot, they say?'

'Yes, sir.'

'When the time comes we may do just that. If we can make a surprise attack then that's what we'll do. But it's best if we can take Bray with no shells falling on the town and killing the local people still there. I hear we had an accident when we retreated.' The captain gave a silent nod.

They were in the general's office in Amiens. It had once been the grand house of the mayor. Now its fine windows were criss-crossed with blast tape and the shining floors scuffed with a hundred army boots.

The general walked from behind his desk and crossed to the door. He stood with his back to it. He looked across at Captain Ellis and winked. 'Who is our spy in Bray?' he asked in a clear voice.

The captain replied carefully, 'If the Germans ever found out they'd execute him.'

'True. But you can tell me.'

Captain Ellis took a deep breath and answered in a loud voice, 'The German spy in Bray is a German officer. He wants to see an end to the war so he is passing messages to us. He takes them to the airfield and one of their pilots drops a message into our garden here.'

On the other side of the door a man with hawk eyes listened then hurried away on tiptoe. His left hand was silver.

Captain Ellis listened to the fading footsteps. 'Do you think our friend Grimm heard that?' he asked softly.

'I'm sure he did. He will pass on the message through his own spy network and the Germans will chase their own tails looking for traitors in their army and air force. Our White Lady spies will be safe.'

Captain Ellis spoke softly. 'We can't let him go on spying on us for much longer, sir. He may be sending real secrets along with the gobbledygook we are giving him.'

General Bruce spread his hands. 'We know he's a traitor. But he's useful. We can feed the enemy nonsense. When the time is right – when he stops being useful – we'll arrest him and execute him. But we need evidence.'

'The girl Aimee heard him pass on the formula for the DM gas, sir,' Captain Ellis reminded him.

'The false formula we invented to catch the spy will confuse the German chemists for a few weeks.' General Bruce chuckled. 'But we just have the girl's word that Sergeant Grimm gave it down the phone.'

'I believe her,' Ellis said. 'And I think he gave himself away when he tried to throw her out of the balloon.'

'*If* he did,' the general said.

'I believe her,' the captain repeated stubbornly.

'I do too. But a girl's word is not enough to execute a man. Give him enough rope to hang himself. Let's wait till the time is right and we will silence the silver tongue of the traitor with the silver hand.'

21 April 1918: Bray

Master DuPont carried a silver-topped walking cane. He didn't need it. He had been carrying messages and walking ten kilometres a day for over two weeks. He was growing stronger and fitter all the time. The cane made him *look* like an old man. When a German passed him in the street or out in the countryside he leaned and bent over the cane and hobbled. He appeared harmless.

Some days there were no messages to deliver so he headed east of Bray into the fields and woods where the Germans had settled. He had a compass set into the top of his walking cane. He measured the distance by counting his steps. When he got home to his little room above the town's hat shop he made a mark on a map to show exactly where each German gun was placed.

On 21st April he visited the airfield and watched new planes being delivered. He made a note of them all, then took his note to the White Lady agent in Cerisy.

Returning home he saw a group of fighters as colourful as parrots flying towards the British in the west. They were led by a red triplane. 'The Red Baron,' he sighed. 'An assassin.'

By the time he'd reached Bray the fighters were coming back to their airfield. The old teacher watched them. There was no red plane there.

He walked up to Colette Fletcher's farm to let her know what he'd done that day. She served him with fresh bread and cheese. 'The White Lady is lucky to have you.'

He looked at her for a long moment then said softly, 'No one else in Bray knows.'

'I will be careful,' she said.

He nodded. 'I know. That's the way it should be. If one of us got caught we'd be tortured and made to tell who else is a spy. If you don't know you can't betray the rest of the group.'

'But you told me,' she said.

He laughed softly. 'There isn't a German torture cruel enough to make you talk, Colette.'

She shook her head. 'No. But I have a weakness. Aimee. If they threatened to hurt her I would betray the whole of Bray.'

'Then my life is in your hands...'

The door to the farmhouse kitchen crashed open and Aimee almost fell into the room. She was followed closely by the German boy soldier who was as pale as ever.

'Maman, Maman, have you heard the news?'

'Calm down, Aimee. Be careful what you say in front of the enemy.'

'No,' the girl panted. 'It was Marius who told me. It's all around the hospital. The Red Baron is dead.'

Master DuPont nodded. 'I saw he didn't land. I thought maybe he'd crashed and was safe.'

'They say the Baron was chasing after a young British pilot when a Sopwith Camel got on his tail and shot him down.'

Marius said something in Latin and Aimee went on. 'But the Baron was flying so low some Australian troops were firing their rifles up at him too. It might have been one of them that shot him. The Baron managed to land on the road from Bray to Corbie on the British side of the lines. When the British got to him he was dead.'

'It will please everyone. We need some good news like that.'

Marius seemed to understand what she was saying. He muttered in Latin, 'It is a sign that we are going to lose the war. He was our Goliath and he has been slain. It makes us sick to the hearts. It makes us want to give up.' Aimee told her mother what he'd said.

'Poor boy,' she murmured. 'He has a miserable life.'

When Aimee returned to the hospital the patients were gloomier than ever. One man began to sing and

the ones who were well enough joined in the old song
'My Good Comrade' about the death of a friend.

'I once had a comrade, you will find no better.
The drum called to battle, he walked at my side,
In the same pace and step. A bullet came
    a-flying,
Is my turn or yours? He was swept away,
He lies at my feet, like it were a part of me.
He still reaches out his hand to me, while
    I am about to reload.
I cannot hold on to your hand, you stay in
    eternal life,
My good comrade.'

As the men sang, Marius whispered to Aimee
what the words meant.

The singing finished.

Silence fell.

Aimee wept.

July 1918: Amiens

The summer days were long. The British army
had to wait until after ten o'clock at night for the
darkness that would hide their stealthy movements.

Their carts edged forwards on roads lit only by the moon. The tunnel of trees that covered the Amiens road kept it gloomy. A man on the back of each cart threw straw on the road. The carts had ropes around the wheels and the axles were greased so they were silent as swans.

They were followed by trailers pulling the tanks they called Whippets. These rolled over the straw so they made no noise. When they reached their positions they were covered in nets and scattered with leaves to hide them. A German spotter plane would not see them.

Not that there were a lot of German spotter planes that summer. Now the Red Baron was gone the British pilots ruled the skies. Any enemy planes that were sent to snoop were soon driven off.

When the tanks were being tested the air force sent up planes to drown out the sound of their engines. The British secrets were safe... except from a spy. But at least they knew who the spy in the camp was. Captain Ellis made sure he had all the secrets the enemy wanted... they were simply the wrong secrets.

The soldiers were trained for the attack. Wherever they went they saw posters saying:

'Keep your mouth shut.'

Another told them:

'If you hear anyone else talking about our plans, stop him at once. The success of this attack – and the lives of your comrades – depend on your SILENCE.'

General Bruce walked into the large dining room in the mansion in Amiens. Fifty men sat there. A cooling breeze drifted through the open windows. Guards stood outside the windows and doors to the room so no spy could hear the plan until General Bruce was ready to leave his false trail.

'As you now know the main attack will take place on 8th August. It will be led by our Canadian friends.'

A large man with a neat moustache looked around the room and nodded. 'Proud to be of service,' he said.

General Bruce went on. 'We expect to take the Germans by surprise. We are sending some tanks and men way up north. The enemy balloon and aircraft spotters will see them plain as day. We'll also let the German spies know that's where we plan to attack... and we'll be telling them the attack will come in September.'

The large Canadian colonel stood up. 'Sorry, General Bruce, are you saying you have spies in the camp and you know who they are? Why don't you just shoot them?'

General Bruce let a rare smile crack his walnut-hard face. 'They are much more useful alive, and telling the enemy our lies. This attack will come as a surprise – so long as you make sure your men keep their mouths shut. Then the Germans won't be waiting to machine-gun our soldiers, shell our tanks or blast our supply roads. Our men will be as safe as we can make them.'

The officers at the table looked serious as they left the room. Captain Ellis gave a silent nod to General Bruce. 'You are an idiot, Captain Ellis. What are you?'

'An idiot, sir.'

'Are you going to keep your mouth shut?'

'No, sir. I am going to sing like a nightingale.' He picked up a green cardboard folder with maps and sheets of typed papers inside. 'I am going to hand this to Sergeant Grimm and tell him to look after it, to keep it safe.'

'What will he do with it?' the general asked quietly.

'He'll pass it on to his friend Benedict, who will pass it on to the Germans.'

'He will. So giving it to Grimm will be a stupid thing to do, won't it, Captain Ellis.'

'It will, sir. But I'm an idiot, sir.'

'Then go and do something idiotic, Captain Ellis,' the general said and his eyes were filled with fire.

'Yes, sir.' The young officer saluted and marched out of the room. In the office Sergeant Grimm was polishing his silver hand and shifting from one foot to the other. His narrow eyes flicked around, nervously. 'Ah, there you are, Captain Ellis. They wouldn't let me into the meeting to take notes for you.'

'No, it was a secret meeting just for the colonels.'

'But I could have made notes and kept a record for you,' Silver Hand said with a small whine in his voice. 'It's my job.'

'No need, Grimm. The notes were all made by the Australians. They're going to lead the attack on 9th September.'

'Are they?' Grimm breathed.

'Ah... sorry... I'm supposed to keep my mouth shut,' the captain said with a silly grin. 'You'll keep *your* mouth shut though, Grimm, won't you?'

'Yes, sir.' That mouth was tight as a rat trap. The small eyes were fixed on the green folder under Captain Ellis's arm. 'Can I put that away for you, sir?'

'Ah, this copy has to be kept safe. Locked away where no one can see it. I need to find a secure place.'

'I can do that for you, sir,' the sergeant said and his hand snaked towards the file.

Captain Ellis clutched it to the brass buttons on his jacket. 'Spies, Grimm.'

'Spies, sir?'

'If a spy got his hands on this the whole plan would be ruined. The Germans would know the Australians will lead the attack eighty miles to the north of here on 9th September. We can't have that.'

'No, sir. So I will put it somewhere safe.'

'The Germans would pay a fortune to get their hands on this.'

'A fortune?'

'Ten thousand pounds – maybe even fifty.'

Silver Hand's voice was a croak. His mouth seemed dust dry. His hand reached forward and touched the file. Slowly, slowly Captain Ellis released it. 'Don't read it, Grimm.'

'I wouldn't read it if you paid me ten thousand pounds,' he said with a creaking laugh. 'Or fifty thousand.'

The young officer slapped the sergeant on the arm. 'Good man. I can trust you to do the right thing with this.'

'You can, sir, oh you *can*.'

And Captain Ellis marched down the corridor to the general's office. Silver Hand muttered, 'Idiot.'

Captain Ellis smiled at the general. 'Idiot.'

22 August 1918: Bray

'My friends,' the mayor said to the people of Bray, who had gathered around the Town Hall steps. 'As you know, the British are on their way back.'

A small, toothless old woman gave a cheer and clapped her twisted hands.

'Shush, Eleanor,' the flour-handed baker beside her hissed. 'The Germans will shoot you.'

'I'm not scared,' she muttered.

'What will you do when they come for you? Bite them?'

Old Eleanor showed her gums to the baker. 'They're on the run. Huns on the run,' she sneered.

The mayor raised his voice. 'The great fightback started two weeks ago.'

'That's right.' Eleanor nodded. 'We've heard the guns. We've seen the sky lit up with flashes bright enough to read a book.'

'I didn't know you could read, Eleanor,' the baker said.

'I can't. But if I could I would have been able to. That's what I'm saying.'

The mayor went on. 'The German colonel came to me this morning and said the British will probably be here tomorrow. His men will fight for Bray. That means the British will be dropping shells and bombs on our town to get the enemy out.'

'The German soldiers were in my shop two weeks ago,' the baker sniffed. 'They said the British would attack in the north in September. Our friends can't be here already.'

Colette Fletcher smiled and whispered to Master DuPont, 'I heard that story too. The British have been very clever.'

'It will rain iron. We'll all be killed,' the fat baker groaned.

'That's why we've been warned,' said the mayor. 'We have time to get out. The British will cease fire tomorrow long enough to let you go west to Amiens. Pack what you can and be ready to leave in the morning. We'll take all the carts and horses in the town.'

'And leave nothing behind,' old Eleanor cried, 'or the Germans will steal it.'

The trembling people hurried away to empty their houses.

Colette Fletcher turned to Master DuPont and said, 'What will you do, Rémi?'

'I have to stay. The British need our reports now more than ever.'

'Your rooms could be hit by British bombs like

Saint Nicolas's church was four years ago. It may be better if you came to our farm. The Germans have painted a large red cross on the roof of the barn to show it's a hospital so the British won't attack it.'

'Thank you, Colette. Let's hope my stay is short. It feels like the war is ending.'

They turned and walked back towards the farm. 'Aimee can hardly remember a time when there was no war,' Colette said. 'Will it really end?'

The old teacher smiled. 'I remember an English saying:

No one lives forever,
Dead men rise up never,
And even the longest river,
Winds somewhere safe to the sea.'

'And you think the sea is in sight?'

'We're on the shore, my dear. On the shore.'

Aimee ran down the path to meet them, her pigtail held in a faded and frayed ribbon. 'The Germans are going,' she cried. 'They're packing up and leaving.'

'So are the people of Bray,' her teacher said.

'Would you like to go to Amiens? To be safe? I have a cousin there you could stay with.'

Aimee looked at him as if he were mad. 'I have the sick and wounded to look after in the barn,' she said. 'It'll be a couple of days before they go. Marius says they're opening a hospital in Peronne to take them.'

'The British will be here soon,' her mother said. 'Then there'll be no soldiers for you to nurse.'

Aimee frowned. 'Yes there will. The *British* soldiers will need my help. Let me stay, Maman.'

Colette shrugged. 'Very well. Your current patients may be the enemy but they are still just people who need our help.'

'That's what I think too. And I can't let Marius down,' Aimee said and ran back to the barn.

The teacher looked at Colette. 'I thought she hated the boy?'

'That was months ago. Things change. In fact I think she'll be a little heartbroken when the lad goes back to Germany.'

But Marius was going nowhere very soon.

24 August 1918: Bray

Bray was burning. From the farm on the hill Colette Fletcher looked down as the old buildings crumbled and tumbled and golden-black flames leaped up to the copper smoke. The shells had stopped now. In the dawn light, shadows of men moved forward over the fields.

The German machine-gunners had gathered in the railway yard to hold back the ribbon of riflemen heading their way. But every time a machine gun fired, the British spotted it and had shells dropped on the deadly gun nest.

Soon the last of the German troops were giving up the fight. They limped through the shattered streets of Bray and headed east and back on the road to Peronne. Others threw down their weapons, shouted '*Kamerad*' at the Canadian troops and gave themselves up.

The last of the German trucks stood outside the barn while sick men were helped on to the crowded seats. Doctor Weger polished his glasses and his face was grey with three days of unshaven beard. 'Aimee, you have been so good to us. Many men are alive because of you.'

'And Marius with his medicine,' she said quietly.

'We will leave just one patient in your care. Marius. So unfair that he should catch influenza now. His temperature is 103. If we try to move him it would kill him.'

'And if you leave him behind he'll be a prisoner. He doesn't deserve that,' Aimee said and sniffed down a traitor tear. 'You go now, Doctor. I'll take care of poor Marius.'

The doctor wrapped his arms round Aimee and the girl pushed him away after a few seconds. 'I am your enemy. We should be trying to kill one another.'

The doctor laughed for the first time in weeks. 'What would be the point? I could shoot you, but you've been so kind I couldn't bring myself to eat you. And I need food more than anything.'

'What are those German words on your belt buckles?'

'*Gott mit uns*,' the thin man replied. 'It means God is with us.'

'Then I hope he'll look after the good men like you,' Aimee said. She turned and ran into the barn so she wouldn't have to watch him go.

Marius had been taken upstairs to the hayloft where he would be well hidden if the British should arrive. Master DuPont had changed him into an old suit of work clothes that belonged to Aimee's father. 'Tell the British he is one of your farm hands... and that if they go near him they will catch flu. That should make sure he is safe till he's better.'

'And then?'

'And then he can follow his friends back to Germany,' the teacher said.

Now the boy lay on the straw, living in some fever-nightmare world of his own. Aimee remembered how it felt. 'My whole body was weak,' she'd told Marius, 'and I'd a headache like drumbeats inside my skull. I was so dizzy I couldn't stand without falling on my face.'

The Germans seemed to have had it worse than Aimee. She had seen so many sick soldiers and heard for herself the hacking cough and seen the trickles of blood dribbling from the mouth. The worst sign was when the face turned blue. She knew that meant death was just hours away.

Marius's face was pale and covered in a sweat but the only colour was the burning red spot on each cheek. No blue.

'Don't die,' Aimee said in Latin.

The boy was mumbling in German. She understood some words now. '*Mutter. Ich möchte meine mutter.*'

'You want your mother, I know. But you'll have to make do with me.'

She sat by his side for hours. She used a damp cloth to cool his brow and fed him some of his own willow-bark drink to ease the fever.

As the sun set and it grew dark in the hayloft his eyes opened and he smiled up at Aimee. 'The doctor?' he asked.

'Gone back to Germany. You can follow when you're strong enough.'

Marius nodded and began to say something when Aimee heard footsteps in the barn below. Then a voice said, 'Set up the radio here.'

She knew the voice. She knew the owner had a silver hand. Aimee placed a finger to the boy's lips and listened as Sergeant Grimm tuned the radio with whistles and whines. She peered over the open trapdoor to the loft.

'Now get out,' the sergeant said to the man who had set up the radio. When the soldier had gone Grimm said, 'Hello? Benedict? Come in, Benedict.'

'I am here, friend,' a voice crackled from the speaker.

'Speak in German, Benedict,' the traitor said. 'Last time we spoke in English that girl was listening. This is her farm. She may be around.'

Then Grimm began to speak quickly and Aimee couldn't understand a word. She heard a wheezing from the boy in the straw. He was trying hard to hold his breath – his pale eyes bulged. At last he could hold it no longer and he coughed.

The stream of words from below stopped.

The two children in the hayloft heard army boots slowly climb the ladder to their hiding place. First a silver hand appeared in the opening. Then the head of Sergeant Grimm, and then a pistol, pointing at them.

'What have we here?' he asked.

24 August 1918: Bray

'This is Robert... the farm hand.'

'What's wrong with him?'

'The Germans used this place as a hospital and left the sickness behind. Robert came into the barn and he caught their flu. I'm nursing him,' Aimee told the man with the silver hand.

Sergeant Grimm shuddered. 'We'll have to swill it out with disinfectant before we take it over for the Canadians,' he said.

'You're too late to save yourself,' Aimee said. 'You were down in the barn for long enough to catch it. I've seen men dead in three days.'

The sergeant's eyes seemed to glow in the gloom and they were the colour of poison. 'You make a habit of putting your snotty French nose into my calls, don't you?'

Aimee glared back at him. 'You are a traitor,' she said fiercely. 'And you tried to throw me out of a balloon to silence me.'

He shrugged. 'But you can't prove any treason. You can't prove I was going to throw you out of the basket. And you don't know what I was saying to my friend just now because we spoke in German.'

Aimee nodded. 'I don't understand German,' she agreed. That could save her life.

But Marius had fallen back on to his bed as he felt weak and the fever returned. 'You're not dead, girl,' Silver Hand told her. 'The disease can't be that bad.'

'The people who've had flu before – a mild sickness – don't get the deadly flu. I'm safe.' She looked at him with a little joy. 'You're not.'

He began to climb back down the ladder. Marius groaned and cried, '*Mutter. Ich möchte meine mutter.*'

The sound of boots on the ladder stopped. They slowly began to climb upwards again. 'German,' Silver Hand said. 'He's German.'

'So? He's harmless,' Aimee said. 'He's a boy. He's sick.'

'He could have understood what I said to Benedict,' the sergeant hissed.

'He's too ill.'

'Better safe than sorry,' the traitor said. 'I'm just going to fetch my rifle.'

This time the boots moved quickly. Aimee hurried over to the boy and shook him. 'Come on, Marius, you have to get out of here.'

Marius groaned and raised himself on an elbow. He rolled on to his hands and knees and began to crawl to the hatch. With Aimee's help he sat on the edge of the steps. She squeezed past him and guided his feet down one at a time. He swayed and almost passed out, then carried on. He stumbled on the last step and fell to the floor, panting and with sweat running into his eyes. Aimee pulled him to his feet, placed his arm round her shoulder and helped him to the door of the barn. The daylight hurt his eyes. It also showed two men walking towards them.

Sergeant Grimm had no rifle. The officer with him had a pistol on his belt. It was Captain Ellis. Silver Hand was jabbering and pointing. 'There they are, sir. The spies. Give me your pistol, sir, and I'll shoot them now.'

Captain Ellis looked at him with some disgust. 'We don't shoot enemy soldiers in cold blood, Sergeant.'

'Ah no, sir, but he isn't an enemy soldier. He isn't in uniform. He's dressed like a French peasant to fool us – to spy on us, sir. Army rules, sir. Any enemy soldier caught *out* of uniform has to be shot.' Silver Hand added in a low voice with menace, 'And you can't break army rules, can you, sir?'

The captain looked unhappy. 'I can't. But he must be executed in the proper manner. By firing squad. At dawn.'

'I can arrange that, sir,' Grimm said eagerly.

'No, I'll do it. It's an officer's job. You have the boy held in the barn and get someone to stand guard.'

'Yes, sir. And what about the girl, sir?'

'What about her?'

'She is guilty of giving shelter to an enemy spy. She has to be shot too, sir.'

The captain was impatient. 'Sergeant, we would need a trial to prove that she helped him. We are in a battle zone. We have more important things to do than set up a trial. The girl lives. The boy will be shot at dawn. The girl is French. We don't shoot our allies.'

Grimm looked disappointed. 'Yes, sir.' He took Marius from Aimee's shoulder and bundled him back into the barn before pulling the wide door shut.

'Now, Sergeant, get back to the old school building. General Bruce needs your help in setting up an office again.'

'I could stand guard here, sir,' Silver Hand said with a soft whine in his voice. 'Give me your pistol and I'd shoot him if he tried to escape.'

'I gave you a direct order, Sergeant,' Captain Ellis said with rising anger. 'Report to General Bruce. If you disobey or question that order you will be tied to the post and shot alongside the boy. Do I make myself clear?'

The man's mouth was tight as a tortoise's. He gave Aimee a look of hatred, turned on his heel and marched down the farm path towards the town where smoke from the smouldering buildings still turned the air thick and the sun dim.

'Are you really going to shoot Marius?' Aimee asked. 'He may be able to tell you what that traitor was saying on the radio just now.'

Captain Ellis looked serious. 'It's difficult. Grimm is right. The law says the boy must be shot. But...'

'But?'

'Look after him. Feed him and get his strength back. I'll send a guard,' Captain Ellis said briskly. 'I'll arrange a firing squad.'

'You can't,' Aimee cried.

The captain's face softened. 'Maybe they'll miss, eh, Aimee? Maybe they'll miss.'

Chapter Four

'While there's life,
there's hope'

25 August 1918: Bray

'I'd like to volunteer for the firing squad, sir,'
Sergeant Grimm had said.

'You want us to shoot you?' General Bruce had
replied with a surprised gasp.

Silver Hand sucked in his cheeks to control his
temper. 'No, sir. I would like to shoot the German spy.'

'You haven't fired a rifle since you lost your
hand. And anyway the Canadians are in the Bray
sector. It's their job.'

'They won't like it, sir,' said the man with the silver hand. 'Men don't like executing an unarmed man – even an enemy. You could trust me to do the job.'

General Bruce's face turned a little red. 'Grimm, I have said no and that's an end to it.'

Grimm swallowed hard, muttered, 'Sorry, sir,' and scuttled from the room.

He had gone straight to the army stores and borrowed a pair of binoculars. Now he stood on the edge of the wood above the Fletcher farm and watched. He had to be sure.

There were twelve men in the firing squad. Riflemen from the Canadian army. They dragged their feet as they marched up the lane to the barn. No one wanted this job.

They formed a line, facing the side wall of the barn. Twelve rifles stood on the ground in front of them. There was a post driven into the ground at the side of the barn with a chair in front of it.

Aimee and her mother stood in the kitchen door of the farmhouse and looked out, grim-faced and grey. Captain Ellis led Marius from the barn. The boy struggled to walk and looked so sick it seemed as if death would be a welcome friend. He had a white patch pinned over his heart. The target. He fell weakly on to the chair and the captain tied a rope round him so he was fastened to the post.

Then he placed a black cloth round the German boy's eyes. Captain Ellis turned and spoke to the stern-faced soldiers. 'This man is a spy. The secrets he passed to the Germans could have got you all killed. So don't feel guilty about shooting him. Don't feel pity for him. He's seen the priest and confessed all his sins.'

'He's no more than a boy,' a Canadian murmured.

Captain Ellis pretended he didn't hear the surly soldier. 'You know how this works. I have loaded two of the rifles with live bullets and ten have blanks. You will never know who fired the shots that killed him. Aim at the square of paper on his chest. Now pick up your rifles.'

The men obeyed, slow and half-hearted. They pulled the bolt back so it was ready to fire. 'Take aim,' Captain Ellis said.

The men raised their rifles to their shoulders and squinted down the barrel.

'And fire.'

Twelve rifles crackled out their charge. Marius's chin fell on to his chest and he sat as still as the barn itself.

'Take your rifles. Right turn... and dismiss.'

The Canadians hurried away, ashamed faces hanging towards the ground. The watching man in the woods saw Captain Ellis step over to the slumped boy, draw his pistol and fire it in the direction of the boy's head. Then he waved at the farmhouse kitchen and an old man stepped out. The schoolteacher. Captain Ellis and Master DuPont walked to the barn, brought a coffin outside and laid it on the ground.

They unfastened the German boy and lowered him into the coffin. Silver Hand watched as the girl and the woman from the farm hurried across the yard to help carry the coffin into the barn.

The men came out and began digging in the rich soil of the farm field. Sergeant Grimm didn't leave his secret hiding place for an hour till the diggers had finished and they had lowered the coffin into the ground.

As the coffin was covered he gave a cruel smile and headed back to the general's office.

In the barn, Marius lay wearily on his bed of straw. 'Thank you, Aimee,' he said.

The girl smiled warmly. 'It was Captain Ellis who set it up and made sure all the bullets were blank. If Sergeant Grimm thinks you're dead then he'll not try to hunt you down and kill you. You're safe.'

'But *you're* not,' he said.

'No, but Maman has an idea about that. She'll explain when she's made us some dinner. Are you strong enough to walk over to the farmhouse?'

'For your mother's mutton stew I'd run there,' Marius laughed.

25 August 1918: The school, Bray

General Bruce closed the door after checking there was no one close enough to listen. The school roof had been damaged when the Canadians took the town and the ceilings had cracked and plaster dusted the floors. Still the army had moved back in.

'So, Captain Ellis, the German boy is safe?'

'He is, sir. He's been very useful. He was pretty sick when Sergeant Grimm called that Benedict but he heard enough to be able to give us priceless secrets.'

'Such as?'

'The main thing this Benedict said is that the Germans are calling our 8th August attacks their Black Day. And they are blaming it on our tanks. They are losing heart for the fight.'

General Bruce gave a tight smile. 'Yes, I watched the tanks in action at Amiens. They just rolled towards the German machine guns and ploughed through them. Wonderful to see. Lots of enemy soldiers just throw away their guns and give up as soon as they see one of our tanks coming.'

'The Germans would give anything to know how to stop our tanks next time. Anything. If Sergeant Grimm can pass on plans of the Mark Five tanks or the Whippet tanks – and show the weak spots – then they will pay Silver Hand and Benedict ten thousand marks each,' Captain Ellis said quietly.

General Bruce nodded. 'Do we have any plans?'

'Yes, they're in the safe.'

'And any notes about weak spots?'

Captain Ellis was almost whispering. 'Yes, we have those too. The men are saying it gets very hot inside the tank. They have to leave hatches open to get enough air. If the Germans use gas shells on the tank drivers the gas will get in and the crew will choke.'

The general shrugged. 'They can put on their gas masks can't they?'

'A tank crew work as a team – they need to work together with the commander to decide which direction to go, the driver to change the speeds, the gearbox men to turn left or right, the gunners to take aim and fire. They are stuck inside a metal box alongside a roaring engine. They have to shout to work together. If they put on gas masks they can't talk. Gas shells will make them almost useless as fighting machines.'

General Bruce nodded. 'I see. The Germans mustn't find that out. Maybe it's time to arrest Sergeant Grimm.'

'We still don't have any proof he's a traitor. And remember he's a bit of a war hero with that silver hand of his.'

The general gave a sharp laugh. 'The German boy heard him speaking to Benedict in German. That's proof enough.'

'Yes, sir, but the German boy is supposed to be dead. We faked an execution. We broke army rules. Even a general could be in deep trouble for that... General.'

The officer rubbed a troubled hand over his moustache. 'So what do we do? We can't let Grimm get away with it... and go on stealing more secrets.'

'No, sir, but the important person in all this is really Benedict.'

'And we have no idea who he is?' General Bruce asked.

'No, sir. We just know he is somewhere near the front line, close to the enemy. He can pass messages across to them. We need to stop him.'

'But we don't know who he is.'

'That's why we still need Sergeant Grimm. He can take us to him. Let's give Grimm plans for the Whippet tank and see where he leads us.'

'And the weakness? We can't tell the Germans that gas will stop the tanks. It may just get through.'

'No, sir, we'll invent something. The Germans use flame-throwers...'

'Evil weapons.'

'Yes, sir. Let's say the tanks will explode if the enemy uses flame-throwers.'

'And will they?'

Captain Ellis almost smiled. 'No, sir. And any enemy trooper with a flame-thrower would have to get closer than ten yards to spray a tank. He'd be shot before he got within fifty yards.'

General Bruce looked troubled. 'So we need to feed Silver Hand with more fake secrets – tank drawings he can't read down the phone – and watch him run with them. You're sure he'll lead us to Benedict?'

'Yes, sir.'

The general lowered his voice. 'And the German boy – the one we failed to shoot? He could cause us a lot of trouble.'

'Send him back to Germany, sir.'

The general sat up straight at his desk. 'Arrange it, Captain Ellis. Arrange it.'

'Send a German soldier back to Germany? It may be tricky.'

The general sighed. He took a printed sheet of cream paper from his desk. 'This is a free pass, signed by me. No one may stop or question the person carrying this. He could walk into Buckingham Palace with it.'

Captain Ellis took the paper, folded it and tucked it into his jacket. He stepped back and saluted smartly. 'Young Marius is as good as in Berlin right now, sir.'

But of course he wasn't...

26 August 1918: The Fletcher farmhouse, Bray

The smell of the smoke from burned Bray still hung in the air. Canadian soldiers repaired some buildings to make garages for their lorries and tanks. They sounded more cheerful now they were moving forward. Their songs hung in the bitter air...

'The general gets the turkey, the colonel has
his duck;
The officers have poultry, they always were
in luck;
The sergeants have bread and cheese and
mop up all they can,
But all the poor old private gets is bread and
Tinker's Jam.'

Captain Ellis carried two backpacks, one on each shoulder, and walked into the farmhouse kitchen.

Colette and Aimee Fletcher sat at the table with Marius Furst. 'I've brought some supplies to help you on the road,' the captain said. 'And inside the front pocket of this backpack there's a letter from the general – with it no one will stop you or question you. But the German army is running fast to the east. You'll have to leave soon if you're going to catch them.'

Marius gave a weak smile. 'He isn't strong enough to go yet,' Aimee said quietly. 'And he doesn't know the way.'

Captain Ellis spread his hands wide. 'What else can I do? I am helping an enemy soldier to escape after we faked a firing squad. General Bruce knows about it but we could all be in trouble if some German-haters back home ever found out.'

'Can't you give him a lift in a lorry?'

'Aimee, I am in charge of spy-catching. I can't whistle for a Canadian army truck to be a taxi for him. No, he'll have to head east alone. The Germans are at Peronne now. If he gets there in

125

two days he can cross no man's land at night and be safe with his friends by morning.'

'What if he gets lost?' Aimee asked.

'There's a map in the backpack.'

'The roads are full of troops and tanks. He'd be better off going along the drovers' road,' Colette said. 'We walk it every year when we take the cattle to Peronne.'

Aimee shook her head. 'I went that way the other day. The road is ruined with the war. If I didn't know the route I'd never have been able to follow the old trail.'

'But you could still find your way to Peronne along it, could you, Aimee?' Captain Ellis asked.

'Of course,' Aimee said.

The officer turned to Colette. 'Would you mind if Aimee went with the boy? To guide him? Only as far as Peronne?'

Mrs Fletcher took a deep breath and blew out her cheeks. 'Of course I *would* mind... but it sounds like it's the only way he'll get back. Marius has helped us. We owe it to him. And it'll keep Aimee out of the way of Silver Hand's revenge for a while.'

Captain Ellis gave a weary smile. That was one less thing for him to worry about. 'I have everything you need here,' he said patting the backpack. 'Maps, compass, good waterproof capes for the rain, a sheet to make a tent at night, matches and a water bottle... and the letter, of course.' He put the bag on the floor by his left foot.

'How will you get back, Aimee?' Marius asked when the girl told him the plan.

Aimee smiled. 'The White Lady members will look after me,' she told him.

Colette nodded. 'That's how I know you'll be safe.' She pointed at a spot on the map. 'There is the village of Cléry. The priest there, Father Gaulle, is one of us. He will see you safely home.'

Aimee smiled. 'It will be an adventure, Marius,' she said.

He gave a feeble nod.

Captain Ellis stood up and said, 'I have to go now. I may not see you again, Marius. Good luck.' They shook hands and the captain made for the door. 'You have two backpacks,' Aimee reminded him and picked up the one that had been by his left foot. She handed it to him.

'Thanks, Aimee. This one is a little trap for your friend Silver Hand. It's plans and a report on the weakness of the Whippet tank – exactly what he wants. I'm going to ask him to deliver it to Amiens.'

'Why?' Aimee gasped.

'He won't go to Amiens. He'll take it to his friend Benedict and they will give it to some contact on the German side. Once he's handed it over, and been paid, we'll arrest them both.'

'It's still a risk,' Colette said.

The officer shrugged. 'I've got a good man following him secretly, don't worry. Nothing can go wrong. Nothing.'

26 August 1918: The school, Bray

General Bruce stroked his moustache furiously. 'I'd like to shoot Sergeant Grimm myself,' he growled.

Captain Ellis stood calmly by the desk in the general's office. 'If we arrest Grimm then Benedict will just find someone else to steal our secrets. We need Grimm to lead us to Benedict.'

The general sighed. 'Very well, send Silver Hand in.'

'Yes, sir.'

The captain walked across the floor of the old school hall. He called through the door to the man with the silver hand. 'The general wants to see you in his office at once, Sergeant Grimm.'

'Yes, sir. Why, sir?'

'Important job.'

They marched in step to the general's office and found him sitting behind a desk. On the desk was the backpack that Captain Ellis had brought from the farm. Sergeant Grimm saluted smartly and stood stiffly with his eyes fixed on a map of the world on the wall, left over from when it had been a school.

'Stand easy, Grimm,' the general said. The sergeant's shoulders drooped but he was still rigid and his eyes narrow with fear. 'Now, I have an important task for you.'

'Yes, sir.'

'In this backpack you have a top-secret document,' he said jabbing a finger at the front pocket. 'It's so secret we can't risk sending it in the usual mail. It has to be taken by hand to Amiens so we can send it back to Britain. There, it will go to the prime minister.'

'May I ask what the secret is, sir?'

'Then it wouldn't be a secret any longer,' the general barked.

Captain Ellis said softly, 'Excuse me, General, but we agreed Sergeant Grimm is the man we trust more than anyone in the British army. If we can't rely on him to deliver a secret to the right place then who can we rely on?'

The general glared at the captain under his bushy grey eyebrows. 'Very well, Captain. I agree Grimm is our top man.' He looked at the sergeant. 'It's about our Whippet tanks. They have a weakness. If the Germans find out before the factories back home put it right... well, the war would grind to a halt. We have to get this message to them as soon as possible. We can't risk a phone or radio call.'

Silver Hand's throat went tight as a turkey's and his voice came out as a strange croaking squawk. 'The Whippet tank, sir. Wonderful machines. They're winning the war for the British.'

'For who?'

'The Brit— I mean, for *us*, sir.'

'There are supplies in the backpack for your journey – food and a rain cape. Go to the mayor's old house in Amiens. Major Green there will give you all the travel documents you need to take the report back to London.'

'You want me to go back to London?' Grimm whispered.

'Of course. Is that a problem?'

'No, sir. My work here...'

'We have another sergeant ready to take over. This is urgent, man.'

'Have I time to make a phone call before I go?'

There was a glint like a steel bayonet in the eye of the general. 'Use my phone.'

'The number I need is in my office,' Silver Hand said.

'Go on, then. Be quick. Take this backpack. Never let it out of your sight. There is a train leaving the railhead heading west to Amiens at noon. Be on it.'

'Sir,' Grimm said. He snapped a salute then reached for the backpack. He picked it up as if it were as delicate as an egg. A golden egg.

When he'd gone Captain Ellis said, 'He's gone to phone his friend Benedict with the good news.'

'What are the chances of his worthless package reaching Amiens?' the general asked.

'About the same as my chances of stopping a Whippet tank with my left foot, sir. He'll be off east and to Benedict as soon as he leaves this office. We have a man ready to follow him.'

General Bruce patted the pistol on his belt. 'I'd still like to shoot him,' he sighed.

26 August 1918: The school, Bray

The phone bell jangled and was answered. Sergeant Grimm spoke quickly in German in a low voice. 'Benedict? I have it. Secret information about the Whippet tank.'

'How?'

Silver Hand explained how they had been given to him by the general and he'd been told to deliver them to London.

'Fool,' Benedict said.

'Yes, the general is a fool.'

'Not the general. You.'

'But...'

'They have set you up. It's all too neat. Who knew you were looking for the Whippet plans?'

'Only the German soldier boy and he's dead. I saw him shot.'

'Then he must have told someone before he died.'

'Probably the farm girl. I wish I'd killed her when I had the chance.'

'It doesn't matter how they found out. The British knew you were looking for Whippet plans and so they handed them to you. They want you to run like a fox so they can set the hounds to catch us both.'

'I have the plans here...' Sergeant Grimm said. He patted the backpack as if his friend could see it.

'They will be phony plans. You still have that key to the general's safe?'

'Yes.'

'Then use it to get the real plans. You'll see they're different. The ones in your hand are fake.'

'I'll call you back.'

Sergeant Grimm tiptoed into the school hall as quietly as army boots would allow. The other clerks were busy with messages and calls. The general had left to meet a French commander. Grimm slipped into the office, opened the safe and flicked through files till he came to 'Tanks' and 'Whippet'. 'Now who's the fool?' Grimm muttered to himself. 'You didn't think I'd check, did you, General?'

He slid the papers inside his tunic jacket then hurried back to his own office and picked up the phone. 'I have them. Plans for the Whippet from the safe. And a note on its weakness.'

'Compare them to the ones they gave you.'

Grimm put his hand inside the bag. 'There are no plans here. Just maps and food. Ellis must have given me the wrong backpack.' He reached into the front pocket and read the paper inside it. His mouth went dry. 'Wait a moment, Benedict.' He read through the letter a second time, just to be sure. He whistled.

'Do you have the real plans, Grimm?' Benedict asked.

'I do. And I have something even better. It's a pass signed by the general. It says that no one may stop or question the person carrying it. Do you know what this means?'

'Yes. You have the real plans... and no one can stop you bringing them to me. Leave now before they know you're gone. You'll be with me in a couple of days.'

'I want to deal with the girl before I leave,' Grimm growled.

'You don't have time,' Benedict shouted. 'If they tried to feed you fake secrets they must know you're a traitor. You need to get away fast. Remember, you may still be followed.'

'Calm down. I have this pass. I can go where no one can follow me. And I can get there as quick as the wind. I may even see you later today.'

Chapter Five

'Life is nothing without friendship'

26 August 1918: The Fletcher farmhouse, Bray

Aimee and Marius had eaten well. Their breakfast had been mounds of scrambled eggs from the farm's own hens on fresh bread, all made by Colette Fletcher.

Aimee's mother added more bread and cheese to the backpack that Captain Ellis had left them. 'Let me see this pass he's given you,' she said and pulled an envelope from the front pocket.

Aimee and Marius looked on as she pulled sheets of paper from a large brown envelope. She shook her head. 'Plans for a Whippet tank... and a note about how it can be stopped by the enemy... using flame-throwers.'

'And the pass?'

'There isn't one,' Mrs Fletcher said with a shrug. 'He must have forgotten to put it in... or he's given you the wrong pack.'

'Should we ask for another?' Aimee said.

'There's no time. You'll have to travel slowly till Marius gets his strength. The sooner you set off the sooner he'll be home. The pass may have helped... but no one is going to stop and question two French peasants. You look harmless.'

Marius smiled weakly. 'I feel harmless.'

'I've put some some money in the pack, and Captain Ellis's map. But you'll not need that. Aimee knows the way. Just stay off the main roads.'

Colette found her eyes filling with tears. She turned away and shook her head. 'Now go. Go quickly.'

Aimee picked up the backpack and walked to the door. Mrs Fletcher turned back. 'And Marius...'

'Yes?'

'When you get home promise me you won't join the army. The first enemy you shoot at could be Aimee's father.'

The boy nodded. 'I won't fight again. When they know my true age they won't let me fight. The war will be over next year, everyone says.'

'Good luck.'

Marius stood as straight as his aching body would allow and gave a sharp bow of the head. Then he followed Aimee into the cloudy day where slate clouds promised rain.

They reached the edge of the woods to the east of Bray and looked back. Mrs Fletcher waved and went back inside the farmhouse.

'We're on our own,' Aimee said. 'Let's get you home.'

Their pace was slow that afternoon. The rutted path was hard to walk on and Marius needed to rest every kilometre. By noon, as he grew more tired, it was every few hundred metres.

The track through the woods was full of shell-holes; the woodsmen's cottages had been destroyed. At every turn they met with sorry ruins, nothing but ruins.

The River Somme sat like a muddy, abandoned ribbon in the valley below them to their right. The roads along its banks were filled with motor-lorries and carts pulled by weary horses. They all struggled across the potholes left by years of battles. Men tried to keep the ruts repaired with gravel but the traffic soon gouged great grooves again.

The woods were little more than splintered trees. An orchard had escaped the shells but the enemy had flattened it as they fled east so the British could not enjoy the late summer fruits.

The young travellers rested and looked from their high ridge across the broken land. The fields were littered with cemeteries and old trenches, shattered villages and deserted concrete shelters that the Germans had left a week before.

A raging storm of fire and steel had passed over the land and left a grey-green-brown patchwork desert.

All the farm animals had gone and rats made the trenches their homes. The girl and boy hadn't spoken much but now the light was fading. 'I'd thought we could shelter in one of the dugouts... but they don't look very healthy,' Aimee said.

They'd reached the line where the British had been a few months ago, before the Germans drove them west. Aimee climbed down a rotting wooden ladder to the floor of a trench. Mouldering boards covered the dark green stinking slime of the mud at the bottom. A light rain began to fall and turned the planks slippery.

Aimee helped Marius down the ladder and a rung snapped. He fell backwards and lay numb for a minute. He was breathing heavily. Then he struggled to his feet, where he swayed, giddy and sick.

'We can't go on much more today,' said Aimee. 'Let's see if there's a dry dugout we can rest in.'

The dugouts were cut into the sides of the trenches and smelled even worse than the trenches. They were overgrown with purple weeds. Aimee pulled a gas-curtain aside and ducked into the darkness. 'Pass me the matches,' she said to Marius. He found them in the pack and lit a candle inside a lantern.

The amber light showed a rough table with papers still scattered over it. The British had left in a hurry.

The earth floor was damp but there were bunk beds made of solid timber and steel plate raised up and dry. They had once had blankets but the rats had chewed them to shreds. A soldier had left a magazine and Aimee read a scrap of a poem. It was one of the comical newspapers that the British wrote themselves.

Aimee frowned as she read it. 'What is it?' Marius asked.

It's a poem,' she said. 'A poem called "The Little Soldiers of the Night".'

'Soldiers of the night?'

'It's not about soldiers... it's about the lice that crawl over their bodies... you see?'

'No.'

'I think it's meant to be funny...'

She read it and tried to explain to Marius what it said.

'The Little Soldiers of the Night
Though some hundreds you may kill,
You'll find there's hundreds still,
For they hide beneath each other
And are smart at taking cover;

Then you have an awful bite,
They've a shocking appetite.

There are families in dozens,
Uncles, mothers, sisters, cousins,
And they have their married quarters
Where they rear their sons and daughters;
And they take a lot of catching,
Cause an awful lot of scratching.'

'I'll take the top bunk,' Aimee said. 'I'm not sure you have the strength to climb up.'

Marius smiled a pale smile and agreed. He placed the oiled rain cape from the pack on top of the damp mattress. The stale air was warm enough so he needed none of the ragged blankets. The dugout smelled of tobacco and rats. He fell asleep moments later.

Aimee lay awake longer, listening to the squeakings and scurryings of creatures that were invisible in the shadows. Marius snored softly. Outside an owl hooted, so she knew that night had fallen. 'Best of luck catching the mice tonight,' she whispered to the owl.

Minutes later she was asleep too.

At the edge of the woods a watcher stood and looked down the hill to the trench where Aimee and Marius had settled for the night. His long black cloak reached below his knees. He took an oilskin from his pack and spread it over some branches to make a simple tent. He lowered himself carefully to the ground. He wrapped his cloak around him and lay there, listening to the rain beating against the roof of his tent.

26 August 1918: The Fletcher farm

Hours before Aimee fell asleep Sergeant Grimm had marched up the path to the Fletcher farm to seek her out. He glanced over his shoulder as if he expected to be followed. He knocked on the farmhouse door and entered before Mrs Fletcher said, 'Come in.' She was sitting at the table, peeling potatoes. The schoolmaster, Master DuPont, sat opposite her. He watched Silver Hand with wary eyes and a forced smile.

'Where's the girl? Little Aimee, isn't it?' the sergeant asked.

'Gone to Amiens,' the teacher said quietly. 'She should have gone back in March when the Germans arrived. Now our town is ruined it's not safe. The Germans could be back at any minute... or they could send bomber planes to hit the railhead.'

Grimm nodded. 'Yes, they'll be back,' he said. 'Sorry to have missed her.'

'Why did you want to see her?'

'Ah... to see if she wanted another ride in the balloon... she seemed to enjoy it last time.'

Master DuPont coughed gently. 'Ahem. An enemy plane nearly blew her out of the sky,' the teacher reminded him.

'Yes... yes... and that spoiled it for her. But the Royal Air Force is stronger now. Since they killed the great Red Baron we hardly see any German planes over the Somme.'

'*Great* Red Baron?' Colette Fletcher said, and raised her fine eyebrows in surprise.

Sergeant Grimm sniffed through his pointed nose. 'One of the rules of warfare, Madame. Respect your enemy. He was a brilliant pilot, a brave man and a noble man too.'

Mater DuPont clutched the edge of the table and pulled himself to his feet. He spoke in a low voice, which the children in his class knew meant he was hanging on to his temper like a child hangs on to a kite in a gale. 'He shot down eighty British and French planes. Some of those planes had a pilot and an observer. So let's say he killed around one hundred of our men. How many wives and mothers have been left to grieve? How many children have been left without a father? He was a murderer and the world is a better place with Baron von Richthofen in his grave.'

Grimm's large ears were red as he flushed. 'You're a teacher. You know everything, I suppose.' He leaned forward so his stale breath blew in the teacher's face. 'When the Germans return you had better keep that opinion to yourself, teacher.' He spat the last word like a pistol shot.

Master DuPont opened his mouth to reply but Colette stood and said sharply, 'Well, Sergeant, you'll be wanting to get back to your duties. You must be busy?'

Silver Hand stood up straight and his small dark eyes glinted in the light from the smoke-smutted windows. 'I have a top-secret message to deliver from General Bruce.'

'Where to?'

'I can't say. It's top secret.'

'Ah. It must be Amiens then,' she said with a smile. 'Maybe you'll see Aimee there? Offer her another balloon ride, eh?'

'I won't see her,' the sergeant said. He spun round on his heel and marched out of the door.

Colette Fletcher looked at the teacher – still shaking with rage – and said, 'He's not going to Amiens.'

'Neither is Aimee,' the teacher said. 'That's what worries me.'

26 August 1918: The road to Peronne

Sergeant Grimm stepped on to the rutted road to Peronne and raised his silver hand, and the steaming lorry stopped. The red-faced driver glared at the man with his backpack. 'What do you want?'

Grimm's eyes narrowed and he pointed to the three white stripes on the sleeve of his jacket. 'I am a sergeant. You are a corporal. You will salute me and ask, politely, how you can help me.'

The driver's mouth looked as if he were chewing a slug. 'Yes, sir. How may I help you?'

Grimm waved the pass in front of him. 'You can give me a lift towards Peronne. This pass says you must give me any help I need.'

The driver smirked. 'That pass might say you're a clown looking for a custard pie in the face... I wouldn't know. I can't read... sir.'

Grimm pulled himself into the passenger seat and said, 'Drive.'

'I'm not going as far as Peronne... sir.'

The sergeant shrugged. 'I'm not going all the way by road. It would take too long. There's a quicker way.'

The driver crunched the gear lever into place and set off. 'Not on these roads there isn't. They're packed. You'll only go as fast as the horse-drawn guns.'

Grimm's thin lips turned down in a sort of smile. 'Not me, driver. Take me to the nearest airfield. There's one down by the Somme, isn't there?'

'Ah yes, sir. It used to be Baron von Richthofen's airfield, they reckon. He's gone now, of course. Have you ever flown in one of those planes? Wood and wire in the wind. You'd never get me up in one of them. Lord, no...'

'Driver.'

'Yes, sir?'

'Shut up and drive.'

The rain began to fall and drummed on the roof of the cab so loud that Sergeant Grimm couldn't hear the swear words the driver muttered.

26 August 1918: The Somme airfield

Sergeant Grimm ordered his driver, 'Stop here,' as they reached the gate to the airfield. Rain was streaming down from clouds that were rooftop low. Mechanics were throwing covers over the engines and cockpits of the planes that stood on the grass runways. The Germans had wrecked the tin-roofed sheds before they abandoned the airfield and flew east.

The lorry skidded to a stop. Grimm opened the door and jumped down into the puddled road without a 'Thank you' to the driver. He showed his pass to the miserable, dripping guard at the gate who pointed to a wooden hut fifty yards away by the fence. 'You need to see Flight Commander Jackson, sir,' he said.

Silver Hand hefted his pack on to his back and bent his head against the driving rain. His boots splashed over the wet grass and he trotted to the hut. He knocked sharply and was told to enter.

He stood at the door and shook off the rain. The commander was a sour-faced, thin man with a deep red scar on his left cheek. 'Army, eh?' he said, looking at Grimm. 'What does the army want with us? More orders for ground support I suppose, eh? Well let me tell you, Sergeant, flying low over the enemy and shooting at soldiers is a dangerous job. We lost two good fighter pilots only yesterday. The German machine guns are waiting for us.'

'No, sir...'

'So where is it this time? Peronne again? Have you any idea how well the Germans are defending Peronne? They're dug in. What do you want? You want our pilots to bomb them?' The commander rose to his feet and leaned across the table that served as his desk. 'Would you like to tell my pilots you want them to risk their lives to do the army's job?'

'No, sir...'

'No, sir. You wouldn't.'

Grimm cut in quickly. 'I mean no, sir, I'm not here with army orders. I'm here to ask for your help. I am on an important mission. I need to get to Cléry and I need to get there quickly. The roads are jammed. It's only ten miles but it could take me till noon tomorrow to get there.'

Commander Jackson looked puzzled. 'Not my problem, Sergeant.'

Grimm gave his small smile. 'I have this pass – orders from the highest command – anyone in the services has to help me.'

The airman's eyes widened as he suddenly understood. 'You want one of my men to *fly* you to this Cléry place?'

'Yes, sir.'

Jackson bared his teeth and shouted, 'Do you think the Royal Air Force is some sort of *taxi* service?'

'No, sir, but orders are orders and you have to help me,' Grimm said quietly with a hint of menace.

Jackson's mouth widened and his snarl became a grin. 'Sadly, Sergeant, I can't fly anyone anywhere. If you were Prime Minister Lloyd George himself I'd have to refuse. My boys can't fly when the clouds are so low, see? You can wave as many bits of paper as you want – you can wave them till you flap yourself into the air – but there will be no more flights till tomorrow.'

'It's urgent...'

'You can sleep in the tent with the mechanics tonight. If I have a plane going to Peronne tomorrow I may let it set you down near Cléry. Now get out.'

Grimm looked angry and disappointed but knew he was beaten. He raised a tired hand to salute and left the hut to find a bed for the night.

26 August 1918: The school, Bray

General Bruce sat back in his chair and groaned. Colette Fletcher sat opposite him quietly. 'So let me get this right, Mrs Fletcher, are you saying your daughter left with a backpack that held fake plans for a Whippet tank?'

She nodded. Captain Ellis stood in the corner of the office, his head bowed and his eyes on the dusty floor.

The general looked at him. 'So our friend with the silver hand has the wrong backpack. And not only that, the real plans are missing from my safe.'

'Yes, sir.'

'It also means he has a pass that will allow him to go anywhere without question. You gave an enemy spy the greatest help possible.'

'Yes, sir.'

'Should I have you shot this afternoon or would you prefer tomorrow morning?'

Captain Ellis knew it was the general's idea of a joke. 'We have a man following him, sir. With or without the pass he'll lead us to Benedict and then we'll destroy the whole spy network.'

General Bruce spoke softly. 'You had better hope so, Captain. Because not only have you helped a spy... you have left Mrs Fletcher's daughter without any help.' The general stroked his thick moustache. 'I am sure Mrs Fletcher would like to be holding a gun in the firing squad when we shoot you, Captain.'

Colette did not join in the joke. 'Aimee will be fine. I wouldn't have let her go if I thought she'd be in danger... well, no more danger than living in Bray. She'll be fine.'

General Bruce answered her but was looking at the unhappy captain. 'Let's pray to God she is.'

27 August 1918: The drovers' road to Cléry

Aimee awoke. It took her a while to remember where she was. Not much light spilled through the gas-curtain over the doorway. 'Marius?' she said. The boy groaned. 'Are you all right?'

Again she just got a groan. Aimee had slept in her clothes. She climbed down from the top bunk and opened the curtain to let in a little light. It had stopped raining and the air was cooler.

In the half-light she found matches and the little stove that the British had left behind. She poured water from her own water bottle into a pan. She would have to fill the bottle again when they reached a fresh stream.

The water boiled and she poured it on some dusty tea leaves from a cupboard. There was a full packet of sugar but no milk. She passed the steaming cup to Marius as he struggled to sit up. 'The sugar will give you strength,' she said.

'Thank you,' he croaked and tried to drink the sticky brew.

'Can you manage five kilometres today do you think?' Aimee asked as she dropped a slice of bacon into the pan, held it over the stove and let it fry in its own fat. The smoke drifted out through the door. She tore a piece of bread from the loaf her mother had given her and prepared to make a sandwich.

Marius sat on the edge of his bunk and held his head in his hands.

A shadow dimmed the morning light. Marius looked up and gave a soft cry. Aimee swung round a moment later and looked into the barrel of a rifle. A German soldier was holding it. His uniform was mud-stained and torn. The man's gaunt face had not been shaved for a week or more and his eyes were sunken pools. He spoke in German and Marius answered quickly. To Aimee he said, 'He won't harm us if we give him our food.'

She held out her two sandwiches and the man pushed one into his pocket and the other between his ruined teeth in bleeding gums. He chewed and muttered. Marius tried to help Aimee understand.

'He says all the men – even the officers – have been eating bread that is as damp as a bath sponge. The food is fried in butter that's as old and rotten as war-fever. They've had to dig green potatoes out of the fields – not new potatoes, but green roots. The flu and the Flanders Fever are leaving us too sick to march or fight.'

'But he's behind British lines. Where is he going?' Aimee asked.

'He says British tanks rolled over his dugout and buried him. By the time he'd dug his way out they had all passed him by. He's going to surrender – hand himself over to the British if we can tell him which way to go.'

'But he could escape back to Germany with you,' Aimee said.

When Marius told the soldier the man laughed till he coughed. Marius nodded. 'He says there is nothing in Germany but hunger and anger. The war is lost. Our soldiers have lost hope. Our troops are thin, the horses have not had a grain of oats for days. The men live on dry barley-bread. But what makes it worse is we know what's coming...

thousands of tanks, tens of thousands of airmen, hundreds of thousands of fit, new men from America.'

'*Es ist fertig,*' the man breathed. '*Wir leben, um den Frieden zu sehen.*'

The boy looked at Aimee. 'He says it's over. All we can hope for is to live to see the peace.'

Aimee walked to the door and pointed towards the woods they'd walked through the day before. With signs she made him understand that was the way he had to go. 'Bray,' she said. 'Bray-on-Somme.'

The man stumbled towards the wood and left Aimee to return and cook a little more of her precious food.

At the edge of the wood the watcher quickly pulled down the tent and rolled it up when he saw the German soldier head up the track towards him. The man in the black cloak had watched as Aimee had pointed the way back to Bray, so he knew the soldier hadn't harmed her.

The watcher hid behind the stump of a shell-shattered tree until he heard the soldier splash past.

27 August 1918: The Somme airfield

Silver Hand woke to the smell of oil and wood, sweat and sausages. The aircraft mechanics were already out of bed and frying their breakfast on a stove in their tent.

He took no part in their talk of sprockets and notches, flanges and cogs, pistons, pipes, pilots and plugs. He chewed silently on the single sausage and bread they gave him.

A flight sergeant came into the tent and pinned a paper list to the tent pole. The mechanics gathered round. 'What's that?' Grimm asked.

'The flights going out today – the pilots, their targets and missions, the planes they'll be flying, the times they're off and which planes we mechanics have to get ready.'

'Any heading for Peronne?' Silver Hand asked.

The mechanic ran an oil-stained finger down the list. 'Pilot Officer Brand is taking an RE8 two-seater over Peronne to drop leaflets at ten a.m.'

'Where will I find this Brand?'

'In the officers' dining hut... but of course you aren't an officer so they won't let you in. You'll have to wait outside. He's a new boy. Young. Fair floppy hair. Went to a very posh private school – talks like there's a tennis ball in each cheek. Nice lad. Bad pilot though. He'll not last long.'

Sergeant Grimm swallowed hard. 'Anyone else?'

'Plenty of fighters heading that way to bomb and machine-gun the Germans... but the Camels and SE5s have only one seat. No, your best bet is with Pilot Officer Brand.'

Sergeant Grimm walked over the wet grass. The clouds were clearing and Sopwith Camel fighter planes were already taking off to scour the skies for enemy planes just as the Red Baron had done, from the same airfield, a few months before.

Carpenters were hammering at planks to build new huts, and lorries were bringing in fuel for the planes as workers patched bullet holes in aircraft, checked the wires that held wings together, tested engines and loaded bullets into the machine-gun drums. No one but Grimm was standing around looking at the muddy waters of the Somme or the watery sunlight struggling through the clouds.

His backpack sat at his feet. He wished he could report on the airfield activity to his German friends. It might earn him extra pay. Maybe it would be enough to simply tell the Germans where the airfield was so they could bomb it.

A tall, fair-haired young man stepped out of the officers' hut. He was as thin as rainwater and his long nose sniffed the morning air. 'Pilot Officer Brand?' Grimm asked.

'That's me. Who wants him?' His voice was rich and slow.

'Flight Commander Jackson said you could take me to Cléry near Peronne this morning,' Grimm lied.

'Really?'

The sergeant showed him the precious pass. 'Oh, I say, top-secret stuff, what?'

'And urgent,' Grimm said.

'Peronne is a battleground, old chap. Not sure I can land you there.'

'It's Cléry village I need to be. That's a few miles away from the fighting. There must be a field you can land in?'

The pilot sniffed down his long nose. 'If our tanks haven't been across it and chewed it to hell, my friend. Can't have my undercart smashed and have you thrown on to your top-secret head, what?'

'Undercart?'

'The wheels. Fragile fellers. Still I'd be jolly pleased to have you along for the ride. We have to fly over the enemy trenches and drop leaflets.'

'Why?'

'Ah, good question. Hang on and I'll fetch them.' He marched off with spider-leg strides and returned with a stack of printed pages. Grimm read them. They were messages to the German troops.

'Sorry.' The pilot sighed. 'They're in German of course... you'll not understand them.'

'I speak German. My grandparents were German,' Grimm said quietly and read on.

Soldiers of Germany

We urge you to give up
Throw down your rifles and come across to
*   our side*
You will receive a warm welcome
You will be taken to a comfortable
*   prisoner-of-war camp*
The food is better than what you eat now
Our guests hold jolly concert parties

You know by now that you cannot possibly
  win the war
The Americans are arriving
Don't risk your life for a lost cause.
  Surrender NOW!

Grimm's face was sour. 'They won't believe these lies,' he muttered.

'Oh but they do. The German officers are so worried they pay the men to collect these leaflets so they can be destroyed. The leaflets are like money... the Huns fight over them. So of course they read them before they hand them over.'

'I see,' Grimm said.

'Come along and I'll show you my bus.'

'Bus?'

'My plane.' Brand led the way across to an aircraft much larger than the Sopwith Camels. The observer sat behind the pilot and there was a machine gun for the passenger to use. The pilot officer pointed to the seat. 'I'll be glad to have you on board. Commander Jackson wanted me to fly over the German positions and throw the leaflets out myself. Of course I can't do that and watch out for enemy fighters, can I?'

'No, sir. Wasn't there an air force observer to do it for you?'

'There *was*... but he didn't make it back from my last trip. An enemy aircraft sneaked up behind us and shot him before I could get out of the way. I mean to say, I heard the chap scream something but the noise of the engine and the wind in the wires made me half deaf. I thought he was screaming because he'd seen a friend called Albert Ross. "Albert Ross," he was yelling.'

'But he wasn't?'

'No. I heard the rattle of a machine gun behind me and turned around. There he was... not Albert Ross. A German Albatross. Silly me.'

Grimm looked shaken. 'He died?'

'He did, poor chap. But don't worry. The ground crew have cleaned up the seat and it's as good as new. Up you get.'

Grimm climbed slowly into the cockpit behind the pilot and took the leaflets. 'Of course you could always drop me off at Cléry before you fly over the German lines,' he said.

'Don't be silly. It's a jolly good wheeze this. We'll be there and back before you can say Jack Robinson.'

'Or Albert Ross,' Grimm replied.

The young pilot threw back his head and laughed a braying, donkey laugh. 'Nice one, Sergeant. You're a funny man. Look, slip that parachute on your back – strap your pack to your front. If we can't land at Cléry you can jump out.'

'No I can't.'

'Nothing to it, old chap. Jump and pull that handle and you'll float down like a dandelion seed. Ready?'

'No.'

'Then off we go.'

27 August 1918: The drovers' road to Cléry

Aimee said, 'Today we'll go just five kilometres.'

'I'm sorry,' Marius said with a sigh. 'I am your enemy. You should not be doing this for me. It is dangerous. I am holding you back. Go home.'

The girl snorted. 'Maman says the man with the silver hand is dangerous. I am safer here than in Bray. Once he leads them to the enemy spies they will arrest him and I'll be safe to go home.'

'Home,' the German boy echoed.

Aimee smiled. 'We'll find this priest in Cléry and you'll be back in your own country soon.'

'What will the priest do?'

'He'll smuggle you through the British lines and get you to your own army. They'll make sure you get back safely.'

Marius managed a weak smile. He struggled to his feet and clutched at the bunk bed till his dizziness passed. 'Five kilometres?' he said.

'We'll stop at every kilometre and rest,' Aimee promised. 'There's an old shepherd's hut on the drovers' road where we can rest tonight. Are you ready to go?' She picked up her pack and carried Marius's too.

They climbed out of the trench and into the grey morning. Marius shuffled slowly and panted. Even five kilometres would be an effort. The land was flat and the rumble of guns from Peronne was faint. From time to time there was the drone of aircraft from the Somme airfield. Some brave skylark rose in the air and sang.

They met no one on the forgotten road. They were fleeing from the man with the silver hand, yet they never looked back. If they had, they might have seen the follower in the long black cloak. He had no trouble keeping up with Marius's slow pace. He hung back. There was no cover on the flat and treeless plain. If they had turned around he'd have had to scramble into a ditch.

So, in that vast flatness, when the aircraft came there was nowhere for Marius and Aimee to hide.

The RE8 plane lumbered into the air with the ease of a winged elephant. Pilot Officer Brand kept low. 'If we climb above the clouds we could be jumped on by a German fighter or ten.'

'And if we stay low the fighters can come out of the clouds,' Sergeant Grimm argued. He'd met enough pilots to know how the war in the air was fought.

'True, old chap. But if I fly above these clouds I might get lost.'

'Great,' Silver Hand said sourly.

They climbed and looked down on Bray. The rains had put out the last of the fires but the streets had black and broken buildings where soldiers like ants tried to keep the roads clear of bricks and beams. Then the pilot turned east. He flew low over the empty plain.

His passenger was looking at the clouds and his one hand clutched at the machine gun that pointed backwards. He was ready to fire at anything that moved.

A gust of wind rocked the plane and Grimm looked over the side to see where he thought he was going to die. He saw a track across the land. Two figures were shuffling along. A girl was helping a boy to walk slowly towards the east.

'He's dead,' Silver Hand groaned. 'I watched them shoot him.' He swung round and shouted to the pilot over the noise of the engine and the rushing air. 'You see those two people on the track?'

'What about them, old chap?' Brand began to circle the plane around the couple. They turned their pale faces up to watch him.

'Fly down and machine-gun them,' Silver Hand ordered.

'I can't shoot unarmed people. They don't look like soldiers to me. Can't kill a couple of helpless peasants in cold blood,' the pilot argued.

Grimm swung the machine gun round and tried to point it at the two helpless fugitives. 'It won't point down,' he raged.

'Of course not. It only fires upwards. Otherwise some careless Charlie would shoot our own tail-plane or wings off.'

'They aren't helpless peasants. They're German spies. If we don't stop them they'll take a pack of secrets to the enemy. Hundreds could die if you don't stop them.'

'Ah, if you put it like that I suppose it's my duty,' Brand said.

He circled again and lowered the nose of his RE8 till the Vickers machine gun was pointing at the frozen figures on the track.

Marius looked at the plane as it circled them. 'It's British. It won't harm us.'

But Aimee was looking at the figure in the rear seat of the plane. A hand rested on the edge of the cockpit. In the weak morning sun the hand shone silver.

'Oh yes he will,' she said quietly and moments later found herself staring into the barrel that meant death for them both. 'Oh yes he will.'

27 August 1918: The drovers' road to Cléry

Pilot Officer Brand raised his eyes, looked over the sights of his guns at the young faces. Suddenly he jerked at the RE8 controls and pulled up the nose of the plane into a steep climb.

Grimm struggled to balance, reached forward and hit the pilot on the shoulder using his silver hand. 'What are you doing?'

'It was a girl,' Brand shouted back. 'And the other one wasn't much more than a boy.'

'Spies,' Silver Hand screamed. 'Spies. You have to kill them.'

'Sorry, old bean, but I don't shoot children.'

'Then land this thing, let me get out and *I'll* shoot them,' the sergeant raged.

Brand's cheerful young face turned hard. 'We have a job to do. Orders to obey. We'll drop those leaflets over Peronne then head back. I can't land here anyway. The rough moorland would smash my undercart like matchsticks. I'll take you back to the Somme airfield.'

'But they're miles east of the airfield. They have a day's start on me.'

'Can't help that. Now get that box of leaflets and prepare to tip them over the side on to the German trenches. We're nearly there. Watch out for enemy planes.'

The pilot climbed again. The only other aircraft they saw were British fighters, who dipped their wings to say hello, then went on their way. Grimm saw flashes from the ground and brown puffs of shells exploded around them as the enemy guns fired at them. 'I'm on your side, you fools,' the traitor muttered.

He gathered the box and tipped the leaflets over the side. They fell like a storm of snow and drifted down towards the pale faces of the troops below. A few machine-gun bullets tore through the canvas of the plane so Brand climbed higher as he turned for home. He looked over his shoulder.

'I reckon we'll be over the village of Cléry in a few minutes. That's where you wanted to go, wasn't it? If your spies were headed east then you'll be ahead of them, won't you? It's better than going back to the airfield.'

'Yes,' Silver Hand snapped. 'Drop me as near to the village as you can.'

Brand gave a gentle smile. 'Here we are... Cléry,' he said. 'Time to drop you.'

The RE8 was a heavy machine to fly, yet the pilot managed to turn it so for a few moments it was flying upside down. Brand had strapped himself into his seat. Grimm hadn't. The roll took him by surprise. He began to fall from the plane. He grabbed the machine gun to stop himself from falling but the stream of air was tugging at him at ninety miles an hour... and he only had one hand... and he had his pack on his front dragging him down. With a hopeless cry his fingers slipped off the cold metal of the gun and he tumbled out of the sky towards the grey-green fields below.

Then he remembered the parachute on his back. He fumbled for the handle on his shoulder and jerked at it. For a few moments it seemed as if the parachute had failed. Then suddenly it opened like a white flower. His fall slowed and the straps tore into his ribs.

He drifted like a dandelion seed but still felt it was too fast to land safely. The ground seemed to rush to meet him. He stiffened his legs to push it away. His right boot hit the ground first and his leg twisted. He felt pain shoot up the leg as something in his ankle gave way.

Then his body hit the ground. The pack with the precious plans broke his fall and saved his face from the damp earth. The parachute was whipped by the wind and dragged him along, painfully fast till it caught in a hedge and collapsed.

Finally he lay still, moaning and hurting but alive. It took him a quarter-hour to gather his wits that had scattered over the cornfield. He managed to unfasten the parachute and sit up.

A cold shower of rain woke him from his daze and he looked around. His pack had come free in the tumble but was lying a few yards away. He struggled to his feet and hobbled across to it. His leg hurt but he could limp through the corn stubble and look around.

The land sloped gently down. He knew Cléry was near the river so if he headed downhill he would find it. Benedict was there, he knew. Benedict would help him recover till it was time to cross the lines to the German comrades who would pay them for their secrets.

He almost managed a smile as he stumbled through a gate on to a rough track. A church steeple in the distance showed there was a village less than a mile away. He set off.

Aimee and Marius clutched at one another as they waited for the plane to shoot them. When it pulled out of its dive and disappeared to the east they sank to their knees – Aimee felt as weak as Marius.

'He could have killed us,' Marius said.

'The pilot could have killed us,' she argued. 'Maybe his gun jammed. Maybe he hadn't the heart.'

Marius nodded. 'What will the man with the silver hand do now?'

'He'll fly back to the airfield and set off after us. He'll be a day behind. There are woods further along this road. At least we'll have somewhere to hide. Can you walk a little further?'

'Of course I can,' Marius said, rising to his feet and trying to hide his trembling legs. Trembling like a deer that was being hunted.

The figure in the black cloak watched them from his place behind the hedge. He breathed heavily. That plane could easily have killed them and there was nothing the watcher could have done to stop it.

29 August 1918: Cléry

The days passed painfully for Marius Furst. He walked a little then rested. The closer they came to the fighting, the louder the roar of the guns. Shell-holes scarred the trail and they filled with slimy, stinking water.

Each evening they stopped when they came to some woods and made camp among the twisted, broken trees. Each morning they woke and Marius said he felt a little better.

They looked into the skies whenever they heard an aeroplane engine but they were never swooped on again.

'Where is Silver Hand?' Aimee said. 'He must have flown back to the airfield. But we're moving so slowly he should have caught us by now.'

'Maybe he's given up the chase. When I get back to Germany I will be a danger to him no longer.'

Aimee looked at him. 'When you get back, are you sure they won't make you fight?'

'No. As I said to your mother, I will tell them my real age.'

'And if they don't believe you?'

'Then I will tell them I am a farmer's son... that my father needs me to work on the harvest.'

The girl frowned. 'They won't let soldiers go home just to look after their farms.'

Marius shrugged. 'But they do. The farm workers go home every summer and come back to fight in the autumn. Germany needs food more than they need men with guns.'

'We still have to get you back to your army. You seem stronger every day.'

Marius smiled. 'I am.' He peered at the map Colette had given them and traced their route with a dirty, broken fingernail. 'Tomorrow we should reach Cléry to find Father Gaulle.'

Aimee reached into her pack and took out the last small pieces of bread and cheese and a withered apple. She shared them. 'Let's hope Father Gaulle feeds us,' she sighed. After their poor meal they lay under their oilskin sheet to sleep a troubled, hungry sleep.

The morning rain woke them. Thunder in the sky echoed the thunder of the pounding guns at Peronne. They set off towards the village.

There were few people on the streets. The rain kept them indoors. But an old woman was watching the new arrivals through the window of her crumbling cottage. Aimee tapped at her door. 'Can you tell me the way to the church, please?'

'No,' the woman replied.

'Why not?'

'Because I don't like that new priest. I haven't been to church since he arrived,' she said, and began to close the door.

'Father Gaulle? What's wrong with him?' Aimee asked quickly.

The old woman's lip curled in disgust. 'He's a German. Are you one of them?'

'No... but...'

'He moved in when they invaded,' the woman said, and her voice was harsh as a magpie's. 'He's stayed on now his comrades have been driven out like rats.'

'So where's his church?' Aimee asked. 'Please.'

The woman jerked a gnarled thumb to her right. 'East end of the village.' She began to close the door again. 'Do you have any food you could sell us?' Aimee asked.

'I have food but not for tramps like you,' the woman growled, and this time her firm push slammed the door.

The rain was heavy and even Marius found the strength to run. The church door was open and they ran through it. The dry, cool air was scented with smoke from the candles that burned near the altar. Two women were kneeling in front of a statue of the baby Jesus in his mother's arms. One woman was weeping, the other just moved her lips in a silent prayer.

Aimee felt she was invading their lives. She and Marius sat silently in one of the wooden pews. At last the weeping woman dried her eyes and rose to her feet. She swallowed her tears and gave Aimee a shy smile. 'My son,' she said. 'He's fighting at Verdun. He needs my prayers.' Aimee just nodded.

'We're looking for Father Gaulle,' she said.

A voice came from the back of the church. 'You have found him,' the man said in a German accent.

'We need help,' Aimee said, turning to look at the priest. He wore a long black robe with a white neckpiece. His hair was white and wild as a dandelion seed. His pale blue eyes sparkled happily as he looked at them.

'Help? Then you have come to the right place.' He walked down the aisle. 'What can I do for you?'

'Marius here is German,' Aimee explained. 'He needs to get back to his side of the fighting. We heard you could help him.'

'Who told you that?' the priest asked.

'My... I mean... a woman. She is one of the White Lady group.'

The priest's thick grey eyebrows rose when he heard the name. 'Ah,' he said. 'I am not one of

178

them – I am German, you see. But they seem to trust me. I work with them from time to time.'

'You do help Germans get home?'

The man spread his hands. 'I help French or British, Germans or Austrians. We pass them from church to church till they get home. We travel at night.'

'How do you get across the trenches?' Marius asked in German. He hadn't followed everything Aimee and Father Gaulle had said.

'A priest leads a small funeral party across from one side to the other. The person we are helping is inside the coffin. Both sides agree to stop fighting to let us pass. A priest from the other side meets the funeral party and takes over. It is very simple. Today is Thursday... I can arrange for you to cross on Sunday.'

'We can't wait three days. There is a man coming to kill us. A man with a silver hand.'

The priest was silent for a long while, then said, 'I will see what I can do. You should be safe here in the church.'

Marius told Aimee what the priest had said. She pinched her lips. 'No. Silver Hand wouldn't worry about finding us in a church. He'd shoot us anyway. He's an ungodly man.'

Father Gaulle sighed. 'What a terrible person. Listen, I have to go out now to visit a sick member of my flock. If you go into the church tower I will lock the door and take away the key. The door is a thousand years old and made of the heaviest oak. It's a safe place. This Sergeant Grimm won't be able to get through before I get back. Come along, quickly.'

They followed the priest's black robes and hurried through the ancient door into the tower. Bell ropes hung over a dusty floor and a wooden stairway led to a platform under the steeple. 'I won't be long,' he said.

Aimee held up her pack. 'We ran out of food last night. Do you have any?'

'I'll bring back as much as you need,' Father Gaulle promised.

The door closed with a boom like doom and the key grated in the lock.

Aimee sat on the bottom step of the stairway and rubbed her tired eyes. 'We'll be safe here...' Marius began.

The girl waved her hand. 'Hang on, wait. What did he say just before we came in the tower? He said something in German.'

'He said we'd be safe. That Silver Hand wouldn't be able to get us in here.'

Aimee shook her head. 'No. He used the word Grimm.'

Marius blew out his cheeks. 'All right, he said Sergeant Grimm wouldn't be able to get us in here.'

Aimee spoke slowly. 'When I spoke to Father Gaulle I didn't use Grimm's name – I called him Silver Hand. Did you tell the priest?'

'No,' Marius said in a hoarse whisper. His eyes met Aimee's. They spoke together. 'So how did he know Silver Hand's real name?'

Marius finished, 'He must know him.'

'And if he's spoken to him recently, Father Gaulle will know about us.'

'Father Gaulle must be Benedict,' Marius groaned.

Aimee looked at the door. 'And this isn't a safe place. It's a prison. We're trapped.'

Chapter Six

'The dead live on in the memory of the living'

30 August 1918: Cléry

Father Gaulle stepped over the puddled cobbles of Cléry and hurried up the slight hill to the farmlands to the north. His black priest's robes flapped around his ankles and his face was set hard as one of his statues. The row of cottages were like a gap-toothed mouth where German shells had landed as the British escaped to the west five months earlier.

The wrecked road up to the ridge had been roughly mended. Smashed gun-carriages, lorries, wagons and cart wheels had not been cleared from the ditches and the fields. They lay twisted and rotting where they had been abandoned.

The priest stopped for breath and looked back. The bridges over the Somme had been blown apart then patched every time one of the armies had fled and the other had followed. Graves with simple wooden crosses were clumped in corners of common land. German and British shared the cold, wet clay.

The farm that Father Gaulle was making for was about the same size as the Fletcher farm back in Bray and the barn was being used as a hospital. This one was full of British soldiers wounded in the fight for Peronne.

There were nurses and doctors hurrying around the men – some groaning, some chatting, some snoring and some too far gone to make any sound. The smell was as bad as any cattle byre and the disinfectant made it all worse.

The nurses didn't seem to notice but Father Gaulle's nose curled up. One of them smiled at him brightly. 'Have you come to give the last rites to the dying?' she asked.

'No, I've come to find a Sergeant Grimm...
I brought him in three days ago to have his ankle
treated?'

'Ah, the walking wounded are in the tents in the
field.'

'Thank you,' the priest said with a small bow.

'Aren't you going to pray for the dying?' the
nurse asked.

'Not today, Fraulein,' the priest said and his eyes
looked sad. As he turned away those eyes became
stone hard again. 'If they are British dying they can
go straight to hell without my help,' he muttered.

Sergeant Grimm was sitting on a cot bed
playing cards with a young soldier, gambling for
matchsticks. He looked up and nodded to Father
Gaulle.

'Good morning, Sergeant,' the priest said in
English.

'Good morning, Father. I hope you are well?'
Silver Hand replied.

The priest didn't have time for polite chat. He
said, 'Sergeant, can you take a walk with me?'

'I can take a limp with you,' Grimm replied with
a sour smile.

'Thank you. Something has come to my church that only you can deal with.'

'What's that?'

The priest shook his dandelion head as if to send a silent message for Silver Hand to talk about this outside. 'Two pigeons have arrived from Bray. They need to be dealt with.'

Grimm's eyes flew wide open and he struggled to his feet. He gripped a walking stick, handed his pack to the priest so he could carry it and hobbled out of the tent. 'The boy and the girl? They're here?'

'I've locked them in the bell tower of my church,' the priest said. He had switched to speaking in German now they were alone.

'I have spent every day watching the road from Bray. How did they get past me?'

'That doesn't matter now. They are here. They need to be destroyed before they betray us.'

Silver Hand tapped the pistol on his belt with his stick. 'It will be a pleasure to shoot them.'

'Not in my church,' Father Gaulle said quickly.

Grimm shrugged. 'Just get your gravedigger to dig two plots. We'll take them into the churchyard after dark and shoot them at the gravesides. With any luck they'll fall straight into the holes and save us a lot of trouble moving them,' the sergeant said savagely.

The two men passed slowly down the road back to the church. Sergeant Grimm talked quickly in a low voice though there were no living creatures but weary cattle and soaked sheep to hear them. 'If we dispose of these two young nuisances we can sell the plans for the Whippet tank. I may even be able to do a bit more damage to the British and French before I cross over to the German side.'

Father Gaulle looked at him from under his heavy eyebrows. 'Are you sure you want to? Germany will be a defeated nation if the war goes on this way.'

Silver Hand laughed. 'No, Germany is setting a trap. They will go back and back till they reach the strongest defences ever built.'

Father Gaulle nodded. 'The Hindenburg Line.'

'Yes, the Hindenburg Line. There will be forts and trenches and tank-traps that the British and their American friends will never break. The only thing they'll break will be themselves. When they are exhausted we will go back on the attack and drive them into the sea for the fishes to eat. It will be a great day for us, my friend.'

They walked slowly along the damp streets where Grimm's stick slipped and he had to lean on the priest's arm. Slowly, slowly they neared the church. A gravedigger was already at work. Father Grimm said, 'We are expecting two new bodies tonight. Not too tall. No need to dig anything too deep either.'

The gravedigger grumbled but said, 'I'll have them ready for you within the hour.'

The priest turned towards the church door where Grimm was waiting. The gravedigger called after him. 'By the way, the slates on the steeple...'

Father Gaulle called over his shoulder, 'Yes I know, a few were cracked when the British advanced through Cléry. I'll deal with it another time.' And he was gone.

The old man stuck his spade into the ground. 'I never did like the Germans,' he spat. 'Priest or not, he'll be sorry when he sees what I saw. Pah.' He pulled out his spade and found a fresh patch of earth to dig two new, small graves.

Silver Hand and the priest walked quietly into the church. Grimm dropped his backpack outside the door and made sure the pistol was loose in its holster.

Father Gaulle took the key from the deep pocket of his robe. He slipped it into the lock, turned the key then twisted the handle. He stepped back quickly in case Marius or the girl was waiting for this moment to attack – perhaps they had worked out his identity by now. Nothing. The priest nodded to the man with the silver hand, who raised his pistol and limped forward.

Grimm entered the gloom of the tower and swept the ground floor with his eyes and his pistol. He looked up to the bell platforms high above. There was nothing but a glimmer of daylight. He backed out of the tower and swung his gun angrily towards the priest. 'They're not there.'

'They have to be. There is no way out.'

'You had them in your hands and you let them slip away.'

'They are hiding somewhere,' Father Gaulle shouted. A woman was lighting a candle near the altar. She looked round in fear when she heard the German voices raised in anger. She hurried out of a side door. 'They will be hiding up in the belfry at the top.'

'I can't climb up there. Not with this ankle. But I am telling you I should be able to see them. There's no hiding place. The tower is empty.'

'It's impossible.'

'Then you find them,' Silver Hand said. He held the butt of his weapon towards the priest. 'Go on in. Take my pistol. You find them, Benedict.'

But Benedict Gaulle – German spy – found nothing.

30 August 1918: Cléry

Marius and Aimee had been trapped in a tower with ancient stone walls as thick as a castle dungeon and a door of oak almost as solid. The lock was dull brass and covered in dust but unbreakable as a jail.

Aimee sank to the floor. Angry at being trapped. Angry that she'd led Marius into danger. She began to sing to keep up her spirits. She sang a bitter British song she'd heard the soldiers sing. It made fun of dying.

'The bells of hell go ting-a-ling-a-ling
For you but not for me:

For me the angels sing-a-ling-a-ling,
They've got the goods for me.
Oh! Death, where is thy sting-a-ling-a-ling?
Oh! Grave, thy victory?
The bells of hell go ting-a-ling-a-ling
For you but not for me.'

'What does it mean?' Marius asked.

'It means hell is waiting for you, my enemy, but not for me. When *you* hear the bells they are the bells of hell. When *I* hear them they're for heaven.'

'There are no bells ringing,' Marius said.

Aimee pulled a face. 'It's only a song, Marius.'

The boy sat down beside Aimee and his eyes glowed in the gloom. 'The bells call me to hell and you to heaven...'

'Yes, but...'

'No. Listen, Aimee. On Earth – here and now – the bells call the people to church,' Marius said.

Aimee grinned. She understood. 'We are in a bell tower. Pull the bell and the church will fill with people.'

'Yes. If the priest and Silver Hand come back they won't dare shoot us in a church full of people.'

Aimee jumped to her feet and dragged Marius up after her. 'You pull the left rope and I'll pull the right.'

They wrapped their hands around the ropes and with a silent nod pulled together.

The ropes stretched down to the ground. There was a small creak. Then nothing. Only silence.

Aimee peered up to the roof. 'There are no bells. There are bell ropes but no bells. Why?'

'One of the armies – yours or mine – took the bells for scrap metal to turn them into guns or bayonets.'

Aimee looked sour. 'Or they took them to make belt buckles that say God is on the side of Germany. The German army have been here for four years. The British just passed through a week ago. It has to be *your* fault. God won't be very pleased if you stole his bells.'

'Then I will be punished if Silver Hand comes back and shoots me,' Marius muttered.

'That's fine,' Aimee said. 'But I don't think it's fair if he shoots me too. I'm getting out of here,' she snapped and walked to the wall where the wooden stairs climbed upwards.

The staircase climbed up the side of the wall in three stages with a landing at the top of each one. Marius panted up after Aimee and had to rest on each landing. When they reached the top, a platform ran around the tower under the roof. 'We can't get out,' Marius gasped.

'Of course we can,' Aimee said. She was growing angrier with every minute that passed.

'The walls are too thick,' Marius argued.

'But the roof isn't,' Aimee said. She pointed upwards. 'Look, the lead has been stripped away.'

'To make bullets.' Marius nodded.

'There are just tiles nailed on... and some of them are already cracked. If I stand on the rail I can push them out. Look...'

Aimee climbed up and stood on the heavy guard rail. She gripped the wooden frame above her head, the frame that had held the bells. If she slipped she'd fall twenty metres to the stone floor below. She swayed. 'If I fall then we'll save Silver Hand a bullet,' she murmured. 'If I fall, make sure you escape.'

As the girl pushed at the tiles they gave way easily and soon there was a hole large enough for her to see the grey clouds scudding across a stormy sky. One tile gave way too easily and she swayed forward. She pushed herself backwards and whirled her arms as she felt herself toppling.

Aimee fell.

As she waited to plummet she wondered if it would hurt or if her world would turn dark in an instant. The song drifted into her mind, '*For me the angels sing-a-ling-a-ling,*' and she knew she'd be seeing those angels soon.

Then Marius grabbed her ankles. She hung off the rail like a trapeze artist she'd seen at a circus in the years before the war. Her pigtail hung down like a little bell rope. When she opened her eyes the world was upside down.

Aimee's legs ached where they were pressed against the rail. The German boy steadied himself. He began to haul her up. Now he was able to grip her knees. The rough rails burned the back of her legs as he hauled her over and at last she fell on to the safe floor.

Marius wheezed like a rusted hinge. After a few minutes he was able to rise to his knees. 'Thank you,' Aimee said quietly. 'You saved my life.'

'So that Silver Hand can shoot you,' Marius said quietly.

'He won't. We're going to escape.'

Marius shook his head. 'We can climb on to the spire but we can't get down to the ground. We can't fly and we don't have a ladder.'

Aimee gave a sly smile. 'And next you'll tell me we don't even have a rope.'

'We don't even have a rope,' he echoed.

Aimee's smile became a wide grin. 'No, Marius. What is your German word for a simpleton? *Dummkopf*? Because we have *two* ropes. The ones they used to ring the bells. They reach all the way to the ground. We put one out of the hole in the roof and climb down it.'

Marius turned red. 'I suppose so.'

'*Dummkopf,*' Aimee teased, and reached out into the void to grab the rope. First she clung on to it as she made the hole in the steeple wider. Then she told Marius to pass their packs, which she threw into the graveyard far below. She gripped the edge of the gap in the roof and pulled herself up. 'Pass me the rope,' she ordered.

The boy hauled the dusty rope up from the tower. It was thick and almost too heavy to lift. It took him five minutes before the bottom end slipped over the rail. He passed it up to Aimee. She pushed the end through the hole and between them they managed to thread it through the gap. At last there was enough heavy rope outside to pull the last ten metres through and it slid through with a rush. Aimee almost fell off the rain-slicked steeple.

She reached a hand inside and Marius climbed up to join her. 'The worst is over,' she said. 'You first.'

The boy stretched his aching shoulders and gripped the rope between his hands and feet. He had climbed ropes in some long-ago time when he had trained in the school gym. That had been a dry, six-metre rope with a soft mat below to break his fall. This wasn't.

He didn't look down. He took a deep breath and slid down carefully.

Aimee climbed out after him. As she rested on the edge of the hole they'd made she heard a sound from beneath them. The door to the tower was being unlocked. If the priest and Silver Hand heard her they would walk out of the church and catch her as she reached the ground.

The rope grated softly against the wood. She held her breath.

The voice of Sergeant Grimm rose up the tower. 'They're not there.' He seemed to be arguing with the priest on the other side of the door. The girl lowered herself carefully and began to slide down.

Marius dropped the last two metres to the soft soil of a grave and moments later Aimee tumbled on top of him.

They hadn't time to lie gasping as they wanted to. They picked up their packs and crept around the tower towards the gate. If Silver Hand stepped out of the church door now he would shoot them.

Yet Aimee lingered on the path. She ran back to the church door as Marius watched on in horror.

She snatched the British army pack that lay there and dropped her own. Then she sprinted down to the graveyard gate and pulled Marius through after her.

'It's Silver Hand's backpack. He has the special pass from General Bruce that we were meant to have. And he'll have food in there too.'

Marius grinned. 'Food. Then the bells of hell won't ring for me just yet.'

They turned east and ran down the road to Peronne.

The old gravedigger watched them go. He looked at the rope and the broken tiles. 'Father Gaulle won't be very happy when he sees that damage,' he said.

He didn't know how unhappy the priest would be.

30 August 1918: Cléry

When Silver Hand and Father Benedict Gaulle stepped out of the church door they saw Marius and Aimee running through the gate and heading east. 'Go after them,' the traitor roared.

'Are you mad? Go after them yourself.'

'I can't run with this damaged ankle.'

'And I can't run down the streets, chasing two peasants, while I'm dressed in my robes. I'd look like a madman. I have to stay here and report on British troop movements. I can't keep spying if the bishop sacks me.'

'We need to stop them,' Grimm hissed.

'Why? We have the plans the Fatherland wants. You can cross the lines and go over to Germany. They will pay you well. When we have won the war you will be a hero.'

Grimm glared. 'Maybe,' he said.

He bent to pick up his backpack. He looked inside and his face turned pale. 'Have you moved my bag?'

'Of course I haven't.'

Sergeant Grimm called across to the gravedigger. 'This isn't mine. Have you seen the pack I left here five minutes ago?'

The old man nodded. 'Those kids took it.'

Silver Hand gave a roar like a wounded bull. 'Our fortune's in that pack,' he groaned.

'Calm down,' the priest said and gripped the traitor by the shoulders. 'Remember what the Bible says... Be strong and brave. Do not be frightened, and do not be dismayed, for the Lord your God is with you wherever you go.'

'Why did the Lord your God let me hurt my ankle?' Grimm spat.

'You fell hundreds of feet from an aeroplane. Your life was spared. The ankle will heal. Those thieving brats can't move fast. Take your time. You will catch them.'

Grimm breathed deeply. Then he hobbled to the church gate. 'They have the pass from General Bruce too. It'll make it harder for me to move through the British lines.'

Father Gaulle nodded. 'You are the same size as I am. Let me lend you my spare robes. If you look like a priest then no one will stop you. I've walked through the British lines many times. They see the dog collar and the priest and not the man. They don't even notice my German accent. Come inside. I will give you the robes and a new pack of food.'

Grimm turned slowly back to the church. Half an hour later he was on his way.

Ten minutes after that a man in a black cloak arrived at the church gate. He rested his cane on a gravestone and asked the gravedigger about two young peasants. The old man pointed the way to the east. As the watcher picked up his cane the gravedigger said, 'And that new priest followed them.'

'New priest?'

'Aye. The Father here's a German. The other one was British, but they seemed thick as thieves.'

'Ah.' The follower sighed and nodded.

'The feller arrived here dressed like a British sergeant then left looking like a priest.'

'Did he now? Thank you.' The watcher set off thoughtfully, his cane clacking on the cobbled road.

'I suppose the Father won't be needing those extra graves after all,' the gravedigger chuckled.

Marius and Aimee struggled against the flow of people shuffling along the road from Peronne. Some were pulling hand carts piled high with furniture. Others had wheelbarrows and prams loaded with their pitiful riches. A tottering old man pushed his crippled wife along in a wheelchair. Sick people hobbled on sticks along the rough cobblestones. Mothers carried babies in their arms. When shells whined over their heads they flung themselves on the ground and sheltered their children with their bodies.

An old woman shivered and clutched her thin woollen shawl about her thinner body. Everything she had left was contained in a small leather bag and she held a picture. It was a photo of a young man in French army uniform. From time to time she kissed it with her dry, cracked lips and muttered, 'My son.'

A poor old man who could go no more laid his few poor goods beside him on the side of the road. He sat with his back to a smashed piano on the pavement and gazed with pitiful eyes at the crowd flowing past.

'Refugees from Peronne,' Aimee said. 'Trying to escape the fighting. Will this war ever end?'

Marius stayed silent. As they climbed the hill back to the drovers' road they escaped the crowd of misery. In the shelter of a few trees they opened Sergeant Grimm's pack and took out some of the food. They ate little because they needed to make it last. 'We reach Peronne tomorrow and then we say goodbye,' Marius said.

Aimee didn't answer directly. She was looking through the pack. She pulled out the plans for the Whippet tank with a note that said it could be stopped with a can of mustard gas. 'These are the real plans,' she said. She began to tear each sheet in half, made a small pile of them, then she took a box of matches from Silver Hand's pack and made a small bonfire of them.

The girl reached into the pack again and pulled out a sheet of thick cream paper. She nodded and gave a small smile. 'This is General Bruce's free pass to anywhere in the British army. It'll be useful.' She looked at Marius. 'Yes, tomorrow we say goodbye.'

Of course, she was wrong.

31 August 1918: West of Peronne

When the sky grew light they struggled out of their shelter and had a small breakfast. They set off on the drovers' road to Peronne again. The main roads in the Somme valley below them were choked with refugees and wounded Australian soldiers rolling west and tangling with army forces moving east, carrying shells and tanks and food and fresh fighting men with their weapons.

Marius looked down. 'When we win the war we will rule France,' he said. 'I will come back to Bray and find you and make sure our rulers treat you kindly. You will be a heroine of Germany for helping me. They'll give you an iron cross.'

Aimee turned suddenly angry as a wasp. 'You will not win the war,' she raged. 'And I am not helping you... you just helped me uncover some spy called Benedict. You are just the bait in a trap. Someone was following Grimm. We have caught your spy.'

Marius sighed. 'I don't know if a spy could follow Grimm. Not if he used a plane to fly to Cléry.'

'Maybe there is no follower, but when we reach the front line *I'll* tell them that Grimm's a traitor and there's an evil priest in Cléry called Benedict Gaulle. They'll arrest him and I will be a heroine of France... like Joan of Arc.'

'She was burned alive by the English,' Marius muttered miserably.

'I would rather be burned alive than wear one of your iron crosses. When *we* win the war, I'll find you and shoot you if my father doesn't come home safe.' She strode off ahead of Marius and he had to trail behind until the drovers' road reached a hilltop and looked down over the river to Peronne.

The low cloud was lit by the flashes of exploding shells and glowed orange-red like the gateway to hell that it was for those on the ground. Yellow clouds of mustard gas rolled across the plain behind the town and a damp westerly wind blew it into the faces of the German defenders.

An Australian officer stood on the hilltop and spoke into a radio, directing the firing of the big guns.

The town of Peronne was covered in smoke and dust as buildings were hit and crumbled. 'What's happening?' Aimee whispered.

The officer looked at them wearily. 'We've been driving the Germans back for weeks. Now they've dug in at Peronne and we're struggling to shift them.'

'Why Peronne?' Aimee asked.

The officer lowered his voice. 'How do I know you're not German spies?'

Aimee gave a light laugh. 'I am a French girl with an English father. Armand here is a simpleton,' she explained, then muttered in Latin to Marius, 'I've told him you're an idiot. Act like it.' She turned back to the Australian and said, 'I'm trying to get him back to his home in Peronne.'

Marius let his face go blank and stared at the sky, which was full of aeroplanes flying east from Bray to attack the town.

'Not today,' the officer said. 'Peronne is on the other side of the Somme there, so the river's like a moat around a castle. The Germans have blown up all the bridges, see?' He pointed to the ruined pillars where they'd once stood. 'When our men try to build new ones they are machine-gunned. We've lost a lot of brave men in those marshes by the side of the river. We put down planks of wood to walk on. They're just half a metre wide.'

The man bit his lip as he lived the pain again. 'Our lads walked into the enemy guns one by one to their deaths. They fell in heaps on those boards or into the marsh and sank. The bravest were the ones who tried to rescue their wounded pals and ended up being shot themselves. That's not a river, it's a death trap. And of course our tanks can't swim across it.'

'What will you do?' Aimee asked.

'We've done it. We crossed the river further down and we're attacking the town from the north side. See?' He stretched out an arm and pointed to a steep hill outside the town to their left. 'That's Mont Saint Quentin... a steep hill the enemy are defending with everything they've got. We started the attack at five this morning. The shells batter the German trenches then our men rush forward to capture the shell-shocked enemy.'

'It sounds simple,' Aimee said quietly.

'Except that the hill is full of shell-holes and slashed trees, it's uphill and the men are already tired from trying to cross the river. Plus we can only spare five hundred Australians to attack nearly two thousand crack German troops.'

'So the odds are against them.' Aimee nodded.

The young officer grinned suddenly. 'Nah... one Australian is worth ten Germans so we have twice as many.' He placed his binoculars to his eyes then handed them to Aimee. 'See? German soldiers throwing their weapons down and putting up their hands. They've lost. Hey, you could be in Peronne in time for supper after all.'

Aimee watched the enemy troops swarm down the hill, hands in the air, weapons thrown to the ground. They were loaded into boats and ferried back across the river to be taken to prisoner-of-war camps. The German defenders in the town couldn't fire at the river now without killing their own men.

Further to the east, on the far side of Peronne, there was a rush of lorries and carts on the road back to Germany. The enemy were fleeing.

'Can we get into one of those Australian boats?' Aimee asked.

'I suppose so. You'll need to cross a lot of old battleground between here and there, though. And of course you're still heading into a battle. You'd have to be desperate to risk it.'

Aimee looked at the main road in the valley below. German prisoners were limping away from Peronne and resting in a field by the roadside. She lifted the binoculars again. Standing at the gateway to the field was a man in a priest's robes over his army trousers and boots. He was talking to an Australian guard. They were too far away to make out their faces. But in the weak sunlight that broke through the smoke of war she could see the silver hand of the British man.

'We're desperate,' she said.

31 August 1918: West of Peronne

The German prisoners sat on the damp grass of the field and ate greedily from the tins of cold beef stew a supply wagon had brought them. Sergeant Grimm marched up to the soldier on guard at the gate. 'Good morning, Corporal,' he said cheerfully. 'A nice bag of enemy soldiers here.'

'Yes, sir.' The soldier leaned forward and spoke quietly. 'If you ask me they look glad to be alive and out of the war. Some of them haven't seen meat for a month.'

Grimm's face turned dark with anger. 'A hungry man is a dangerous man, Corporal. They can still win this war. Now get back to your regiment.'

The man blinked in surprise. 'I've got to guard them till their transport gets here.'

Grimm sniffed. 'I've been sent to relieve you.'

'Are you sure, sir? You're a priest.'

Grimm pulled the priest robes over his head to reveal his sergeant's uniform. 'A disguise. I dress as a priest to fool the German prisoners and get them to talk to me about their battle plans.'

The man shook his head in wonder. You don't have a rifle...'

'I have a pistol. These men won't give me any trouble.'

'But your hand, sir...'

'I fire my pistol with my right hand,' Grimm snapped. He raised the silver hand in the air. 'I got this saving an officer under heavy machine-gun fire. Do you think I can't manage a few defeated men with no weapons? Well? Do you?'

'No, sir. Sorry, sir,' the corporal said. He saluted smartly and marched out of the gate and joined the crowds of men plodding towards the battle.

Sergeant Grimm turned to the prisoners and spoke rapidly in German. 'My friends, you are heading for a prisoner-of-war camp in France.' The prisoners looked at one another in surprise. Silver Hand went on. 'But there are two types of camp. The good ones where you get food like this every day. You'll get Tickler's Jam, fresh milk and eggs and the best doctors to care for you. But there are evil camps for the prisoners who behave badly. The food is potato water and turnip skins, the work is hard and the huts are cold.'

The Germans looked suspicious. Why was this man telling them this? They soon found out. 'There are two young peasants on the run from Bray – a German boy and a French girl. It's a bit like Romeo and Juliet, you might say. But the French girl's father is a general and he wants her back. If any man can capture them he will be treated like a prince. I have tracked them to the hills a mile from here. But my ankle is slowing me down and they are slippery young people.'

A German sergeant rose to his feet. 'Why doesn't the general use a squad of British soldiers to catch them?'

Silver Hand sneered. 'Because he would be thrown out of the army. Imagine it? Using fighting men that are needed for the war just to catch a couple of young runaways? No. I am his assistant and he's given me the job. I am offering you the chance to have a comfortable life in your prison camp. What do you say? Is anyone willing to help me?'

The prisoners muttered among themselves. It seemed too good to be true – was it a trick or a trap of some kind? Their sergeant asked, 'Will we be armed?'

'No need. They are two young people. With thirty men I can surround the moorland and catch them and destroy them.'

'Destroy them?'

'I mean... return them to where they belong. Destroy their foolish plan to escape back to Germany.'

The German sergeant looked around. 'Are there any of you willing to give it a go? I'll do it? Anyone else? Stand up.'

Slowly the prisoners began to rise to their feet. At last they were all standing. There were around fifty of them. 'Excellent,' Grimm said and made a fist of his good hand. 'Follow me out of the field and on to the moors.'

As they set off the German sergeant turned to Grimm and said, 'You speak good German.'

'I was brought up in Wales but my parents were German.'

'And yet you fight against us?'

Silver Hand gave a sour grin. 'Yes, but not very hard.'

'Your hand? You are a hero.'

Grimm limped along and murmured, 'I was opening a tin of soup. The opener slipped and I cut my hand. It turned septic and the doctors had to amputate it. I made up the story of my gallant rescue. It helps. People like a hero. I get away with a lot more than an ordinary sergeant.'

The German gave a harsh laugh. 'I think I could like you. Let's get Romeo and Juliet, shall we?'

31 August 1918: West of Peronne

On the moors to the west of Peronne there wasn't enough cover to hide a cat.

As the afternoon sun burned, the clouds melted and the area was flooded with light that made the fleeing couple stand out. The open moorlands were prison walls, and the war-scented air of death was like a breath from a forgotten dungeon.

Down the slope, a couple of kilometres away, the German soldiers formed a curving line that was sweeping round to make a circle.

Silver Hand limped along and fell behind but he could wait. The fit German soldiers would do his work for him.

'Can you run, Marius?' Aimee asked.

'Not for long,' the boy replied. 'You head for safety. If they capture me then don't worry. You've done your best. Run, Aimee, run.'

Aimee's face turned red with fury. 'How dare you tell me what to do?' she demanded and gripped him by the shoulders.

'I thought...'

'We've been together for months. Haven't you learned I don't give up easily?'

'Yes, but...'

'You want me to abandon you to save myself? Did *you* abandon those sick soldiers when they had flu and save yourself? Or did you risk catching the sickness and letting it kill you?'

'Yes, but...'

'You saved a hundred lives. I can save one.'

Marius finally managed to get in a word. 'They were my comrades. You want to save an enemy.'

Aimee pulled a face. 'Yes but a feeble one who wouldn't shoot a Frenchman if he had a dozen machine guns.'

'Thanks,' Marius muttered.

'Now we only need to get to the top of this ridge. They will see us clearly against the sky. I will run west as if I were running back to Bray. You go over the hill and head east down to the River Somme where they're crossing. I'll join you in an hour or so. They'll follow me because they will see me running along the ridge.'

'But if they see you they'll catch you,' Marius said as they climbed to the top of the crest. They stumbled over shell-holes. When they looked back the searchers were closer now... less than a kilometre away and striding out.

'They won't catch me if I run fast enough,' Aimee said. 'Take my backpack and I'll fly like a swallow.'

She handed the pack to Marius and he panted to the top of the ridge after her. He looked down on the crowded river below and across to Mont Saint Quentin. 'Three broken bridges,' Aimee said quickly. Meet me at the one in the middle.'

Marius crouched down so he could look back down the hill they'd just climbed. When he turned back he saw Aimee racing across the long ridge, pigtail streaming behind her. Angry German voices were carried on the west wind.

But she was right. The line of fifty followers had swung around to follow her. One man broke away from the line. A slim, young soldier who was fitter and faster than the rest. He headed along the bottom of the ridge. If he got to the drovers' road before Aimee he'd surely cut her off or drive her back into the arms of the other hunters.

It was a fair race. Aimee in her light boots running along the top. The soldier in his clumsy uniform keeping pace with her along the bottom. The young man threw off his helmet, then his belt and his jacket.

There was a wood a kilometre ahead. Aimee talked to herself as she ran, the beat of her words keeping time with her flying legs. 'Reach the woods. Go to earth. Hide beneath a fallen tree. Let them think I've run back home. When they're gone I'll double back. Look for Marius. Cross the Somme.'

Then she remembered she wasn't supposed to cross the Somme. This was where she'd say goodbye to the boy. She'd use General Bruce's letter to make sure the boy got a passage on a troop carrier. He'd have to catch up with the fleeing German army without her help.

But thirty of the German army were after her at the moment. The young soldier was definitely closer – half a kilometre now... maybe less. Four hundred metres.

His comrades were baying like hounds after a fox. She didn't understand all of the German words though she'd learned a little in her time with Marius. But she knew what they meant. 'Get her.'

The soldier reached the head of the valley and now he just had to climb up to meet the path that Aimee was running along. He'd cut off her escape. His worn boots began to slip and he had to avoid shell-holes full of muddy slime. He was panting hard now as the poor German army food had left him exhausted.

Still he was there. He was two steep steps from the top of the path. He flung himself across the path. Sprinting, Aimee saw him reach out a bony hand to grab her ankle as she sped past. Aimee jinked to one side then jumped over his legs like a hurdler. The soldier snatched and missed. He fell face down on to the spot where her feet had been an instant before. The force knocked the breath out of him. He struggled to his feet and took a while to pick up speed again.

The soldier paused. He wiped the sweat from his eyes. Aimee was gone. Ahead of him was a broken clump of trees. She could be anywhere – hiding or running through. She would hide, he decided.

He waited in his sweat-stained grey shirt for the troop of Germans to catch him.

Before the war Aimee's father had hunted deer and rabbits in the woods on winter weekends. 'It's poaching,' he said. 'And if I get caught I go to prison.'

And when the gamekeepers arrived to trap him he said, 'If you are surrounded on all sides in a patch of land there is only one chance of escape. You mustn't run for it. Stay in the one place, let your enemies search it and not find you.'

That worked for him, but how was she to escape notice in that postage stamp of a place? She burrowed beneath the trunk of a fallen tree where angry beetles scurried out of her way, and pulled ferns across to cover her.

In the quiet of the damp and damaged wood she heard the murmur of men speaking. Then one voice rose above the rest. It was the voice of the man with the silver hand. 'Search every inch of this wood, under every branch, every twig, every leaf.' Again she didn't understand all the German words but she knew what he was saying.

A man in a black cloak, carrying a cane, and with his face shadowed by a hood walked towards the searching men.

'Good day, Sergeant,' he said in English.

'Good day,' Grimm snapped.

'May I help you?' the traveller asked politely.

'Not unless you've seen a young girl with a pigtail on your travels.'

'Ah,' the hooded man cried. 'She passed me ten minutes ago.'

'Where?'

'On the road to Cléry. I was climbing the road to this wood and I saw her run in then run out the other side. She looked afraid and very tired. I watched her run all the way down the hill. She seemed to be looking for somewhere to hide in the hedgerows. Is that the girl you want?'

'It is,' Silver Hand said. 'She's a runaway. We're finding her so she can get safely home to her mother.'

'Ah,' the hooded traveller said. 'Then I am so happy to have been of some help.'

Aimee heard Sergeant Grimm give new orders and the German prisoners moved off and onwards to Cléry. By the time she slipped out of the woods, and headed east again to find Marius, the stranger was nowhere to be seen.

She didn't know who he was. She did know his lies had saved her life.

31 August 1918: Peronne

Aimee opened her pack and took out the letter from General Bruce. She showed it to the Australian soldier who was in charge of loading the boats across the Somme to Peronne on the east bank. 'See? We can go anywhere and you have to help us.'

The soldier pushed his helmet back a little and rubbed his head. 'But the battle isn't over.'

'The Germans are running away,' Aimee argued. 'We saw it from the top of the ridge.'

'I know. But they have snipers... sharp-shooters with rifles. They hide behind any tree or building or shell-hole and shoot our men when they try to follow.'

'They won't shoot us. We're not in your army. We look like refugees.'

'But you're not?' the soldier asked.

Aimee had found Marius waiting for her by the landing stage. They smiled at one another when she arrived safely. But they both knew they had to cross the river before Silver Hand discovered his mistake and came after them again.

'We are in the White Lady group.'

'You look a bit young to be spies.'

Aimee sighed. 'We are messengers. My mother is a member in Bray. This boy speaks perfect German. He can mix with the enemy and report back to us.'

'Why would he do that?'

'Because he's from Austria. His family hates the German people.'

The Australian soldier watched a wagon bringing wooden beams and metal girders to repair the bridges on the far side. He guided the men as they lifted the materials off the lorry and on to the barge. Other boats of all sizes were landing with prisoners and wounded troops and the odd group of refugees who had lost their homes in the fighting. 'So can we cross?' Aimee begged.

'When it's loaded you can find a corner on this barge,' the soldier said. 'You'll be there in half an hour.'

Aimee explained what was happening to Marius. They looked back up to the ridge. There were no sign of their hunters. But in half an hour they could still arrive.

At last the barge was ready to leave. Marius and Aimee perched on an oak beam and felt the boat rock as the sail was raised, and it made the short trip across. At that moment the sun glittered on the hand of a man who stood at the top of the ridge above the river. The man with the silver hand must have seen them for he threw both hands in the air in rage.

'Good luck,' the Australian soldier called as the barge drifted away from the shore.

'If a man with a silver hand asks to cross then stop him,' Aimee cried. But most of her words were swept away with the rumble of guns, the hammers, saws and axes of the bridge builders, the shouts of soldiers working or the cries of the wounded being unloaded.

'A brass band?' the Australian laughed. 'Crazy kids.'

And Sergeant Grimm began to limp down the hill to find a boat.

They hadn't escaped. They had just slipped through the hunter's net for a little while.

As the boy and girl hurried through Peronne they were unsure where to turn or where to hide. Half the houses had burned and were still smoking and the choking air stung their eyes and throats.

Most of the others had lost their roofs and none had any windows.

'We could stay in one of the ruined houses,' Marius said. 'Maybe he'll go past and miss us.'

Aimee shook her head. 'Not for long. I did that in the wood at the top of the ridge. He won't fall for it again.'

They reached a fine house near the centre of the town. Its walls seemed strong but there was no roof. Smoke dust drifted from the windows where there had once been glass. A woman was trying to drag a wooden chest on to a cart that was pulled by a donkey. 'Can I help?' Marius asked her with the little French he had learned from Aimee.

The woman was aged over fifty, with thick face make-up and deep-red lipstick. Her hat and coat looked expensive and she even wore silk stockings. 'The servants have all left me. We were sheltering in the cellar when the shelling started. As soon as it was over they cleared away the rubble and set us free. I thought they'd help me move my precious things. But what did they do? They loaded some sticks of furniture then ran off to find their families.'

Aimee tried not to show a sour smile as she said, 'Poor you.'

'I can't stay here... and I can't go without my treasures.' The woman looked sharply at Marius and Aimee. 'Not treasures... not gold or jewels. Just things that are precious to me. Things like...' she began, then stopped.

'Photographs?'

'Yes, photographs,' the woman lied.

'Ornaments? Letters and diaries?' Aimee went on.

'Exactly. I mean, I am not a rich woman. But if you help me load this trunk on to the cart I'll reward you.'

Aimee grabbed one end of the wooden trunk and Marius the other. 'Put it on the seat so I can sit on it to drive the wagon,' the woman said.

They did as she asked. 'Heavy photographs,' Aimee muttered as the coins in the chest rattled. Aloud she went on, 'Where are you going?'

'I have a country home in the woods near Hirson. The Germans are being driven back. I'll follow our armies till I get to my other home.'

'That's halfway to Germany,' Aimee explained to Marius. To the woman she said, 'Marius here would make a good servant. He can look after the donkey... protect your treasures from bandits on the road...'

'Bandits?' the woman screeched.

'Yes. German bandits. Enemy soldiers who've deserted their army and live by robbing refugees like you.'

'I am not a refugee. I am just going for a summer holiday. I am Madame Clare and no one would dare attack me.'

Aimee just spread her hands. 'If you say so, Madame Clare.'

The woman's crimson mouth turned down as if she'd supped on vinegar wine. 'But there would be no harm in the boy coming along. And you could come too... mend my clothes, cook my meals, wash my undergarments.'

Aimee was about to say, 'I would rather die,' when she saw the man with the silver hand at the end of the street strewn with rubble. He was asking a dust-stained policeman some questions. Aimee spoke quickly. 'Yes we'll do all of those things, but only if you can get us out of Peronne now. There is a man chasing us because he thinks we stole some secret plans.'

'Stole? You're thieves?' the woman hissed.

'No, we are heroes of France. He's a British traitor. But we need to get away. Let us hide on your cart amongst the furniture. If you get us out of Peronne we'll see you safely to Hirson.'

'I can't pay you,' the woman said quickly.

'We'll work for free. We'll be better than slaves. Just get us out of here.'

'Hide in that wardrobe,' the woman said.

Marius scrambled on the cart after Aimee, slid under the canvas cover and crouched inside the wardrobe. They closed the door on a darkness that smelled of mothballs.

September 1918: The road from Peronne

The wagon creaked and moved. Peronne smouldered like a dying ember while poison gas hung from the trees like tinsel.

Aimee peered through a crack in the door of the wardrobe. They were in a train of refugees. Some heading east to return to their homes now that the German invaders were leaving. Some following the armies in the hope of making money or finding work. She was sure no one else was heading towards a summer home in the forests of the east, like Madame Clare.

But there was no sign of the man with the silver hand, trailing behind like a shadow of death.

For a moment Aimee thought she had a glimpse of the man with the long black cloak and the walking cane. The man who had saved her as she hid in the wood. But she blinked and he had disappeared.

'You should go home now,' Marius said as he stepped out and joined her.

'It's as dangerous to go back as it is to go forward. I could walk into the arms of Sergeant Grimm. I'll stay another day,' she said.

That day did not take them far. When the army needed the road the refugees had to pull on to the dusty verge and let the soldiers march past followed by their supply lorries and tanks and guns. Now the Australians were singing happier songs. They knew they were winning and driving forward.

'We soldiers of Australia
Rejoice in being free,
And not to fetter others

Do we go o'er the sea.
Old England gave us freedom,
And when she makes a start
To see that others get it,
We're there to take our part.'

Then there was their song 'Waltzing Matilda' with the words changed. Hard men with skins like old leather sang like schoolboys and laughed as they marched and sang about the German king, the Kaiser...

'Fighting the Kaiser, fighting the Kaiser,
Who'll come a-fighting the Kaiser with me?
And we'll drink all his beer,
And eat up all his sausages,
Who'll come a fighting the Kaiser with me?'

Aimee was never sure when it would be safe to leave the convoy. So she stayed. 'I'll go as far as Hirson and meet up with a White Lady there,' she told Marius. The days rolled slowly by.

The donkey cart rocked over the hills that were as fat as sheep, just a few kilometres every day. At night Madame Clare tried to find a tavern to stay in. Aimee and Marius squeezed into the crowded cart and slept under the canvas. On fine evenings they slept under the stars.

News spread among the travellers about the war. Every day that September it seemed the British and Australians were moving ahead faster and further than the refugees could.

Each day the guns seemed more distant. The autumn hills less damaged by the battles. The air less scented by the gas. The nights less infested by rats. The villages less crushed by shells.

Madame Clare said she was poor but she used the chest as a driving seat and sat on it to guide the donkey. No one could look inside. She always seemed to have enough money for the best food when they came to a farm or village. Aimee grew fond of the donkey, Daisy, and made sure she was well fed though Madame Clare grumbled about the cost.

Marius slowly grew back to full strength and was useful in heaving the cart out of muddy patches when the hard black rains fell on the rutted roads.

One day they came across a field filled with rough huts and British officers with bright brass buttons on their tunics and hats. 'A new command post,' Marius said.

Aimee slipped away from the wagon and used General Bruce's pass to get past the guards at the gate. She asked the way to the command room where phone lines hummed and Morse code keys clattered. She persuaded a signalman to send a message back to Bray to let her mother know she was safe and would be away longer than she planned. And she told her about Father Gaulle's link with the treacherous Silver Hand.

When the reply came through an hour later Aimee was back on the road and never saw it. The message said, 'I know you are well. A friend is sending me reports. We have heard about Father Gaulle and are taking action, but beware the man with the silver hand. He is a still a danger. When you get to Hirson find the local priest. He is a friend of the White Lady. He will help. Love Maman.'

On 26th September, at Saint Quentin, the enemy stopped, turned and battled back, just as they had at Peronne. Madame Clare's cart almost caught up with the fighting. They could smell burning wool on the breeze. That was the scent of the mustard gas.

There was no more sleeping under the stars. The sky over the battlefield, in the evenings before and after dawn, was aflame with exploding shells, star signals and burning fuel dumps, and the villages glowed amber-gold and gave off showers of silver sparks. It was all too beautiful and terrible. They rested in the village of Attilly where Madame Clare found an inn to sleep in.

That night the heavy rains returned. The canvas over the wagon leaked. Marius and Aimee found a barn to shelter in. There were the usual rats but a family of cats kept them away from the sleepers.

The barn was like Aimee's own in Bray and the cats like the one back in the school. For the first time Aimee felt a sick longing to go back home.

Then, when morning came, Marius found the bombs.

Chapter Seven

'Laws are silent in times of war'

27 September 1918: Attilly

In the early morning light of the barn Aimee woke and saw Marius was already exploring the place. He saw her rub her eyes and sit up on the straw that had made her bed. 'This was an old ammunition dump used by the German army,' he said.

'The German army?' Aimee said with a frown. 'Don't you mean *your* army?'

'I suppose I do,' Marius said. 'I don't know what I am any more.'

'What have you found?'

'A box of grenades... they explode five seconds after you pull the pin out.'

'We've shared the barn with a box full of bombs?' Aimee muttered. 'Maybe I was wrong when I said I'd be safer travelling with you.'

Marius shrugged. 'There's a blue cross on the box... that means they are a poison gas ... it makes you choke, sneeze and cough if you haven't a gas mask on.'

'Nice.' Aimee snorted. 'So we wouldn't have been blown apart in our sleep, we'd just have been gassed?'

'They are safe until you pull the pin out,' the boy said as he took three bombs from the box and stuffed them into his backpack.

'What are you doing?' Aimee demanded.

Marius explained. 'When Sergeant Grimm was chasing us...'

'What do you mean? When? For all we know he could *still* be chasing us. He could be waiting outside,' the girl raged.

Marius smiled quietly. 'And what will he do?'

'Take his backpack away then shoot us.'

'And how will we defend ourselves?'

'We can't. We have no weapons and you can't fire a gun and... Oh, I see,' Aimee said, her voice falling away as she felt foolish.

Marius nodded. 'I tell him the plans are in this pack. I reach in and pull the pin. I hand the bag to him... slowly. Five seconds after the pin comes out the gas bursts from the bag. If I time it right it'll blow just as he opens the bag. He'll be blinded and choking for days.'

'And if you time it wrong he shoots us,' Aimee said bleakly.

'He's going to shoot us anyway. At least this way we have a chance.'

Marius fastened the bag and they set off to Madame Clare's wagon. She was waiting for them and looking as cross as ever. 'Hitch up Daisy, boy,' she said to Marius. 'And you, girl, light the paraffin stove and make me some acorn coffee. It's awful stuff but better than nothing. I've had my breakfast,' she said. 'The innkeeper found me some fresh eggs on toasted white bread. It cost me my last penny, of course, but it may get me through till lunchtime.'

'Don't worry about us,' Aimee said sweetly as she lit the small tin stove. 'We caught a rat and ate it. All except the tail. It should get us through till Christmas.'

'When we get to Hirson my gardener should have this summer's crop of vegetables stored safely in the pantry and meat in the ice house. If you work hard for me you'll eat well.'

'Oh thank you.' Aimee sighed. 'We are like Hansel and Gretel, lost and alone. And you are the owner of the gingerbread house, come to our rescue.'

'I am,' Madame Clare said... forgetting that the gingerbread house was owned by a witch.

The rain was heavy that day and Marius climbed down to help Daisy pull the cart through the stretches of road that had been churned and turned into a sticky pond. Lorries skidded past and turned the boy into a walking statue of clay. They travelled just a kilometre by noon; it was a midday that was as dark as midnight.

Madame Clare made sure her treasure box was locked then disappeared into a roadside tavern for lunch, carrying the bag that she took everywhere.

She was there a long time. Aimee took Daisy out of the shafts to give her some food and let her nibble grass in a field.

At last Madame Clare appeared, looking restless and excited. 'There is no point in struggling on today,' she said. 'The army is held up at Saint Quentin and the roads are blocked with lorries that have slid into ditches. Pull the cart into the field with Daisy and we'll stay here till the weather clears.'

'There's a drovers' road just over the hill,' Aimee said. 'We need to keep moving.'

Madame Clare's face turned red under her pale make-up. 'We stay here. That is an order. Don't disobey me, child. We stay here.'

Aimee bit her lip to stop her angry reply. 'Yes, Madame,' she said.

'I'll wait in the tavern. You stay here.'

As she turned to go something fell from her bag. It was a piece of folded paper.

Aimee was so cross she said nothing as it floated down into the mud. 'Serve her right if it's precious,' she muttered. Then she stepped out of the shelter of the cart's canvas roof and picked up the sheet. She unfolded it and her face turned grey as the clouds.

'What's wrong?' Marius asked.

'It's a small printed poster,' Aimee explained. 'A sort of Wanted poster. It says General Bruce's daughter has been abducted by a German spy... It describes me, and it describes you.'

'You are not the daughter of General Bruce.'

'No. It's just a story to make people think we're worth reporting. And that we are worth a thousand francs reward.'

'There is a price on our heads... like outlaws?'

Aimee nodded. 'And it gives a number to call. It asks anyone who sees us to call the church at Cléry and report to Father Gaulle.'

Marius thought about it. 'Silver Hand is on the road behind us. Whenever he has the chance he'll call Father Gaulle and ask if there've been any reports.'

Aimee nodded. 'And look at the roof of the tavern. See? By the corner? There? That wire?'

'A telephone line,' Marius said. 'Madame Clare has betrayed us.'

'Sold us for a thousand francs,' the girl agreed.

'That's why she was in the tavern so long.'

'And that's why she wants us to stay here. She wants us to wait till Sergeant Grimm comes and captures us.'

'We have to leave. Get your backpack,' Aimee said briskly. 'We'll head up to the drovers' road. He'll never track us there.'

Marius hurried to the tail of the cart. He climbed down and looked back down the road when he heard the roar of an engine. A hawk-eyed soldier in a rain cape was leaning out of the hatch of a Whippet tank, giving orders to the crew of drivers and gunners inside. The soldier looked up and saw Marius a moment later.

'I think it's too late, Aimee. Silver Hand's already here and he's seen us. We're dead meat.'

Aimee gripped Marius by the shoulders and shook him. 'We can go across the fields,' she shouted over the noise of the rain beating on the canvas. 'He didn't catch us before when you were almost too weak to walk.' She began to drag him to the field gate where Daisy stood with streams of water dripping off her drooping ears.

'But in this mud we'll be lucky to do five kilometres an hour. I looked at that report on the Whippet tank. I didn't understand much but I did see some figures. I am sure they said a Whippet can go at eight kilometres an hour... and it doesn't need a rest. We can't run at eight kilometres an hour.'

Aimee grinned in spite of the danger. 'No, but Daisy can. Hurry.'

Inside the Whippet tank the air was hot and thick with exhaust fumes. The crew were in their vests to cope with the heat. The engine noise was painfully loud and the men wore leather helmets with their earflaps pulled down. There was a gunner at one side and two gearsmen at the back. They had to change the speed of the tank tracks to make it turn. The driver sat at the front and tried to see his way through the driving rain.

Sergeant Grimm dropped into the spare gunner's seat and shouted over the din, 'Head left into that field. I can see the runaways.'

The driver gave the order to the gearsmen and the tank slowly turned. The wooden gate was closed. The tank turned it into splinters and churned through the mud into the field.

Silver Hand looked out through the gun port and saw his prey climbing on to a donkey. He pushed back the catch on the machine gun.

'You're not going to shoot the girl, are you?' the driver shouted.

'I'm going to bring down the donkey then kill the boy,' Grimm replied. He looked along the barrel of the machine gun and pulled the trigger a moment after the front of the tank dipped into a fold in the field. The bullets sprayed the earth and sent up clods of damp grass.

When the nose rose up again the tank was facing uphill but Marius had steered Daisy to the right, towards a small woodland. It had a few broken trees but gave a thicker cover than most of the war-torn woods in the area and the tank couldn't follow them in there. The donkey had heard the gunfire and broken into a canter for the first time in her life. The trees were close now.

'Right, right, right, turn right,' Grimm screamed and the driver passed on the order to the gearsmen. But by the time the runaways were back in his sights they were vanishing into the trees. Silver Hand pulled the trigger. A tree crashed down and made a barrier that even a tank couldn't cross.

'Turn left – go around the wood and we'll catch them coming out of the other side,' Grimm ordered.

The Whippet tank turned and began to run around the outside of the wood.

In the wood Marius slowed the donkey to a walk. 'Hurry,' Aimee urged him.

The boy slid to the ground and handed the reins to her. 'We might get a head start on Grimm when we're out of the wood but we could still be in range of that machine gun. We have to stop the tank.'

'You're mad,' she said.

'Didn't you say a Whippet crew had to have lots of air vents so they could breathe in all the heat?' Marius asked as his fingers were busy with the buckles on his backpack.

'Yes. That's why they can be stopped with a gas attack.'

Marius nodded and pulled out a grenade. 'That's just what I have here.'

'But as soon as you get near they'll shoot you,' Aimee argued.

'Only if I stand in front of the thing. And if they kill me at least it'll give you time to get away. Good luck.'

Before Aimee could argue any more, Marius was running along the path through the trees. When he reached the edge of the wood he saw it opened out on to the rough moorland beyond. The tank was just coming around the outside of the wood. He threw himself behind the thickest trunk he could see.

The tank reached the place where it crossed the path. Silver Hand pushed up the hatch to see if the runaways were on the road ahead or still in the wood. While he was at the hatch Marius knew he couldn't be firing the machine gun. The boy sprinted towards the tank. When he was two seconds away he pulled the pin. In another second he had rolled the grenade under the tank. He had two seconds to turn and get clear.

Sergeant Grimm was screaming something in English. Probably a curse, Marius thought as he dived under the cover of a fallen log. There was a soft bang. Then just the steady thudding of the tank engine as the machine stood in the rain. Then shouts of panic from the men inside as a yellow gas cloud wrapped around the machine.

There were whirring gears and hot exhaust pipes with no guards on. The half-blind men had to leave the steel mantrap slowly and carefully or risk losing a hand in the gears or skin on the scalding pipes.

The two hatches flew open. Five men, weeping and coughing, fell on to the ground. They splashed their hands in the long wet grass to rub water into their swollen and red-lidded eyes. Some simply buried their faces in the grass and lay there coughing. Only Silver Hand rose to his feet and turned his sightless eyes to the sky. He shouted in German, 'You will die slowly for this, boy. But first you will watch your little friend die even more slowly.'

'*Gott mit uns*,' Marius called back before he turned and ran from the tentacles of gas that were slithering over the ground to choke him.

Madame Clare looked shocked. She stood by her cart and watched Marius and Aimee walk down the hill towards her, leading Daisy.

Marius began to fasten the donkey into her harness while Aimee gave the woman her sweetest smile. 'You must be surprised to see us,' she said.

'I thought you had stolen the animal and run off,' the woman said in a choking voice.

'No, you thought we'd been captured by the British army. You were waiting for your reward. You tried to sell us, Madame Clare.'

The woman's face suddenly turned sly and soft. 'I thought I was returning you to your dear father who is missing you so much and...'

'... and the thousand francs was not important? Don't lie, Madame.' Aimee stood nose to nose with the woman and spoke quietly. 'Marius here is a crack German fighter. He used Daisy here to lure the British into the wood on the hill and he killed them one by one. Now he is going to kill the woman who betrayed us.'

'No,' the woman moaned. 'I have money. I will pay you.'

Aimee gave a sad, understanding smile. 'Marius took some grenades from the British dead. Marius, show Madame Clare the grenades.'

The boy opened his pack and showed her the two gas grenades.

Aimee went on. 'They are powerful enough to blow open your treasure chest. We can take all of your treasure any time we want. But we are not thieves, Madame Clare. All we want is to be paid

245

fairly for our help. At the next town you will stop and buy us some new clothes. Our boots are as thin as paper and winter will soon be here. We want warm coats and stockings and hats and oilskin coats. Is that not fair?'

The woman's mouth set in a hard line. 'It's fair.'

'Then let's go.'

Daisy was harnessed and fresh in spite of her race up the hill. As they'd walked back down from the wood to Attilly, Aimee told Marius she had never been this far on the drovers' road and didn't know the way east. Anyway, when Silver Hand and the tank crew recovered their sight they would set out down that moorland road looking for then. The best plan was to keep travelling with Madame Clare on the main roads. It would be crowded and blocked from time to time. But they'd have food and shelter and look like a family, not a pair of runaways.

The wagons set off from Attilly towards Saint Quentin. News spread like a spilled oil-lamp fire that Saint Quentin was being taken by the Australians. To the south the Americans had joined the war and were driving the Germans back.

It was gloomy news for Marius. Aimee said, 'If it means an end to the war by Christmas then it's good.' The boy just nodded.

29 September 1918: Attilly

Father Benedict shook Sergeant Grimm warmly by the hand. 'You have done well,' he said.

Silver Hand rubbed his eyes, still sore from Marius's gas grenade from two days before. 'I think the game is up, Benedict, my friend. We need to get across to the German side even if we don't have the Whippet tank plans. At least we can tell them a gas shell can knock the tanks out.'

They sat in the bar room of the tavern at Attilly. The landlord came to collect the empty plates from their mutton stew. Benedict looked up at him. 'Did you see that woman with the two runaway kids?'

The red-faced, sweating landlord glared. 'I had the posters up but I never went outside. I didn't know she had those kids with her when she asked for a room.'

Benedict smiled like one of the angels in Cléry church he'd left behind. 'Of course you didn't. How could you? No one is blaming you, good sir.'

The man gathered the empty plates and gave a silent nod. 'But what can you tell me about the woman?' Father Gaulle asked.

The landlord shrugged. 'A snob. She had a sharp tongue. Spoke to me like a servant. Wanted the sheets on the bed changed because she said they weren't clean enough. They'd only been washed a week before. She said that at her home she had fresh sheets every day. I feel sorry for her servants.'

'And did she say where her home was?' Silver Hand asked.

'Her house in Peronne had been wrecked by shells so she was going to her summer home as soon as the Germans were cleared out of the area.'

'And her summer home is where?' Father Gaulle asked.

'Hirson, she said. About fifty kilometres to the east of here. She set off two days ago.'

'Did she buy a new donkey?' Grimm asked sharply.

'No, she had the same old donkey she called Daisy.'

The sergeant's eyes widened. 'Then the runaways must have brought it back. Maybe they are still travelling with her.'

'To Hirson at least,' Benedict said softly. He took a bundle of francs out of his pocket and placed them on the table.

'That's too much, Father,' the landlord said.

Benedict grinned. 'It is worth every sou.'

He hurried Silver Hand to the door. 'You're right, we need to get to Germany. But on the way we can go through Hirson.'

'They have two days' start,' the sergeant reminded the priest.

'So we need to move quickly.'

Silver Hand frowned. 'On these crowded roads? Even if we had a lorry we wouldn't catch them.'

'No, but a horse could. We can go cross-country to Hirson, find where this woman lives and be there waiting for them. I will go to the local church in Attilly and ask to borrow horses. I'll say it is God's work. *Gott mit uns*, my comrade. *Gott mit uns*.'

October 1918: the road from Saint Quentin

The October winds were spiteful but among the ruined streets of Saint Quentin they found a shop with the clothes they needed.

Madame Clare spent the days that passed in her sulk. Whenever she argued about opening her chest to pay for good food or clothing then Aimee tapped Marius's backpack with the grenade inside.

At the town of Benoite, Aimee found an army base and sent a message back to her mother. This time she waited long enough for a reply. 'Captain Ellis's men went to arrest Father Gaulle in Cléry but he had vanished. They think he is going to join Grimm and flee to Germany on the same roads you are travelling. They are still a danger. You are being watched over, so I know you are safe at the moment. But your watcher has lost sight of Grimm. When you get to Hirson look for the priest, Father Raoul. He is a true member of the White Lady and will help your friend cross to the German lines. Love Maman.'

Aimee remembered the man with the walking cane and the black cloak. From time to time she looked back and thought she saw his shadow in the shadows.

'Fifty kilometres to Hirson and Madame Clare's home,' Aimee said to Marius after she had looked at the army maps. 'The enemy are still falling back. It could take us a month to get there. But when we do, there's someone there to see you safely home,' she promised.

'Home,' Marius murmured.

Chapter Eight

'Friendship is tested when bad luck strikes'

6 November 1918: Hirson

The British army moved forward steadily. The Germans were sick and war-weary. Some troops stood and fought. Some threw down their weapons and decided their war was over. All they wanted was the silver hand of peace.

As the British moved forward the two German spies followed. The sight of Sergeant Grimm's uniform and Father Gaulle's priestly clothes meant no one stopped them in the fog and fury of war.

At last, on 6th November, the German forces were driven out of Hirson and Sergeant Grimm and Father Gaulle rode into the town.

The town had not been damaged. The German retreat had passed through quickly. Grimm and Gaulle went to the town's best tavern and found rooms before British officers could take them all.

The wind was icy now and the two men huddled around a log fire in the bar room. 'I asked in the grocer shop and learned this Madame Clare lives in a large house in the woods a mile north of the town,' Silver Hand said. 'The house is still empty, except for a gardener and his wife. The grocer says the gardener has had an order from Madame Clare. She'll be home tomorrow with two new servants.'

'We can guess who the servants are. Tomorrow they will breathe their last,' the priest said.

'The girl and the boy have seen us both. They've run away from us before and they'll do it again as soon as they see us.'

'Then you'll have to stalk them like you would a tiger. Hide in the trees and shoot them before they see you. I have a feeling their luck is about to run out,' Father Gaulle said.

'You aren't going to help me?' Grimm asked.

'I'll be with you, as ever, my friend. In at the kill, as the British say,' he said coldly.

Daisy seemed to pick up her hooves and trotted happily when she knew she was near Hirson. The skies were cold and grey as zinc and there was the scent of snow in the air. When Madame Clare reached her home she seemed a different woman from the sulky one who had spent her money on warm clothes for Aimee and Marius. Her voice was shrill once more as she told her gardener the house wasn't clean enough.

The old man was a gnome with a bent back and a face creased like linen. 'Sorry, Madame, we've not had any ready water for the past week. The rope in the well snapped. The bucket's down at the bottom. My wife's had to walk a kilometre to the stream to fetch water for cooking.'

'So mend the rope, stupid man.'

The gardener sighed. 'I'm too old to go climbing down wells, Madame. Sorry, but if I went down I wouldn't be able to get back up.'

'Then it's just as well I have a fit young boy with me.' She turned to Marius. 'You, boy. Go down the well and fetch the bucket to the top. And you, girl,' she said to Aimee, 'take a pail to the stream for some fresh water. We crossed it on the way up here.'

Since they'd left Attilly over a month ago, they were rested and well fed. Marius would soon be home and it seemed the war would be over before Christmas. They didn't mind repaying Madame Clare with a little help before they left.

Marius went across to the well and found there were iron rungs hammered into the inside wall. Aimee hurried down to the bottom of the hill where a stream ran across the road. The men riding down the far bank looked at first like two soldiers as they wore heavy British greatcoats. One man was wearing a pair of gloves. The other needed only one glove. He didn't need one on his hand of silver.

As soon as she saw them, Aimee dropped the bucket and sprinted back up the hill. The horsemen kicked their horses into a trot and followed. Aimee ran through the front gate, looking around wildly for Marius. Madame Clare came out of the front door and snapped, 'Where's the pail of water?'

'Where's Marius?' Aimee demanded.

'Getting the bucket out of the well,' the woman said sourly.

'Two men on horses... looking for us... don't tell them where we are. Say we ran off into the woods,' the girl panted before she raced to the back of the house. She ran across to the well and called down, 'Marius? Hurry. Silver Hand is here.'

'How near?'

Aimee could hear the clatter of the hooves on the front path. 'Twenty seconds at the most.'

'Then I can't make it. Save yourself,' Marius shouted back.

'I've come this far,' Aimee said. 'I'm not leaving you now. She climbed on to the wall of the well and began to go down the iron rungs. 'He'll never find us in here,' she said. 'Once he's ridden off we'll get out and escape,' she whispered. The whisper echoed around the stony walls of the well.

Silver Hand was sure he had his prey this time. 'If they run we will hunt them down on our horses,' he told Father Gaulle. 'It really is over.'

The priest smiled and turned towards the woman at the front door. 'Good day, Madame. We are looking for a runaway couple.'

Madame Clare said nothing but stared hard. Sergeant Grimm went on, 'I believe you reported them back in Attilly, did you not?'

She gave a single nod.

'So where are they now?' the priest asked.

'You were offering a thousand francs reward back then,' Madame Clare said. 'You didn't pay.'

'They got away,' Silver Hand said. 'But now the reward is double that.'

'Show me the money.'

The sergeant reached inside his greatcoat and pulled out his pistol. He pointed it at Madame Clare. 'What's your life worth, Madame?'

She swayed and clutched at the door to steady herself. 'The boy's in the well.'

Silver Hand grinned. He turned to Father Gaulle. 'Stay here with the horses, Benedict. Watch this woman.'

He climbed down from the saddle and walked quietly around the side of the house to the back garden. He stopped at the well, leaned over and listened. He could hear the whispering. 'I know you are down there. I am going to count to five. You will come up or I will shoot you where you are.'

'Then you won't get the tank plans,' Aimee called up. Silver Hand blinked with surprise. So the girl was down there too. Perfect. Two mice in one trap.

'I will search the house till I find them. That woman won't stop me.'

'We've hidden them,' Marius said.

'Then we have a deal, my young friends. You come up and show me the plans. I will spare your lives.'

'He's lying,' Aimee muttered to Marius.

'I know. But it's the only chance we have,' the boy sighed.

Aimee shifted her hands on the rungs and pushed herself upwards. 'We must stall him,' she said. 'Distract him and make a run for it. It's only twenty metres to the garden fence, and then we're in the woods.'

'Let's hope he's a bad shot,' Marius muttered and began to climb.

They were five metres from the top when Aimee froze. She heard the priest's voice as he walked across the garden to the well. 'Madame Clare showed me their backpack. There are no Whippet tank plans in it. They must have destroyed them.'

'They say they've hidden them,' Grimm said.

'They haven't had time, the woman says.'

As Aimee looked up she saw two heads appear and block out the light from the dismal, cloudy sky. 'Then we may as well shoot them now,' Sergeant Grimm said.

Aimee heard the safety catch on the pistol click and watched as the man pointed it down towards her. She closed her eyes.

There was a soft thumping sound, then a cry from the priest and another thump. Silence. She opened her eyes and looked up. The two faces were gone. In their place was a single head, shrouded in a black cloak. A hand reached down and as she climbed up it grasped hers and helped her out. Marius followed and they looked in wonder at the scene.

Silver Hand and Father Gaulle lay stretched out on the grass, crumpled and still. The stranger in the black cloak had a walking cane in his hand. It had a heavy silver handle and he was gripping the cane by the tip. He'd used the handle to club the men to the frosted earth.

The stranger reached up and pushed back his hood. Aimee looked at him and a slow smile spread across her face. 'You are the last person I expected to see here,' she said.

9 November 1918: Hirson

'You followed us all this way?' Aimee asked the man with the hooded cloak.

'You mother asked me to,' Master DuPont said. 'I lost sight of you from time to time. But every village has a member of the White Lady in it somewhere. They were looking out for you and they always put me back on your trail. And the pilots from the Royal Air Force flew over every day and their observers dropped me notes whenever they saw you... they told me where both you and Grimm were. But I was almost too late getting here,' he said.

Aimee threw her arms round her old teacher and hugged him. 'I am so pleased to see you. You saved our lives.'

'Thank you, sir,' Marius added and shook Master DuPont's hand. 'Will you take Aimee home now?'

'We have two fine horses at the front of the house. We can thank Father Gaulle for them.'

'What shall we do about Grimm and the priest?' Aimee asked. 'Kill them?'

The old teacher shook his head. 'We are none of us killers,' he said. 'We need a day's start to get Marius across the border and get ourselves on the road home. No, we'll tie them to the well and tell Madame Clare not to set them free for twenty-four hours.'

'They'll freeze,' Marius said.

'That would be a shame,' Aimee said.

The groaning and groggy pair were tied securely with rope from the garden shed. Master DuPont led the way past the pale and frightened Madame Clare. 'They are spies,' he told her. 'And if you set them free before tomorrow morning you will go to prison for a very long time.'

They walked the horses back to Hirson where the old man led the way to the church and met with the White Lady contact there. Father Raoul, the priest, was wrinkled like an ancient apple but willing to help. 'Yes, a brother called Father Gaulle told me to expect a German refugee coming to cross to the other side. What was his name again? Something to do with fairy tales, I seem to remember.'

'Grimm?' Master DuPont said. 'You are due to help a German called Grimm to cross?'

'That's it. Grimm. See? I'm not losing my memory. I have a permit to take a dead German across to the other side so he can be buried in his home. All the paperwork is correct. So this young man is called Grimm, eh?'

'Yes,' Aimee said quickly.

'Come back here at midnight,' the priest said. 'We'll pop him into a coffin and four strong men will carry him over. Once he's in the church on the other side they'll set him free.'

'Thank you, Father. We'll be back at midnight,' Aimee said.

They hurried into the town centre, hunched against the cruel wind. They walked through the crowds of British soldiers marching east. 'We're so close to the German army but there isn't the usual roar of the guns,' Aimee said.

'No, there's not much fight left in the Germans now,' Master DuPont explained. 'The harder they fight the more chance the Germans have of being killed in a British revenge attack. They're keeping their heads down. They say there will be peace next week.'

They ate well in a tavern near the town, where Master DuPont decided to stay the night. As the town hall clock chimed midnight Aimee and Marius were walking up the path to the church, the wind whining through the gravestones.

The inside of the church was lit by two lanterns. In the gloom there stood a black coffin. The lid was open. Marius seemed to tremble a little as he peered into its dark red satin lining. The four coffin bearers and the priest stood in silence.

Aimee bit down on her lip. At last she trusted herself to speak. 'We can go home now.'

'I owe you my life, Aimee,' Marius said.

'You saved mine back in Attilly,' she replied. 'I guess that makes us even. Now get in the coffin or I'll take Master DuPont's cane and knock you out.'

'You'd do that too,' Marius said with a lantern-lit shadow of a smile. 'After all, we are enemies.'

'We are,' Aimee said. 'But you are a good enemy to have. You went to war and hurt no one. You saved a hundred lives with your medicines.'

'And you hate me still?'

'Of course. Until the war ends. I hate you Marius Furst,' she tried to say but the last words were lost as she choked back tears. Suddenly she stepped forward and threw her arms round him. They held one another tight for a minute. The old priest gave a gentle cough. 'We are expected on the other side, Master Grimm,' he said gently. 'Time to go. Time to say goodbye.'

'Goodbye forever?' Marius asked Aimee.

'Forever is a long time. Who knows,' she said and ran from the church.

11 November 1918: East of Hirson

Sergeant Grimm and Father Benedict Gaulle walked up to the general in charge of the front-line troops. Grimm was still raging that Father Raoul had told him he'd been carried across the night before. 'There will be no more rescues now. Tomorrow the war will be over,' the priest of Hirson explained.

'By tomorrow the British military police could have arrested us,' the sergeant said. 'We'll have to take a chance. Walk across.'

Father Gaulle nodded. 'If peace is arriving soon, they won't shoot a couple of priests. Put the robes on.'

The spies walked towards the front lines of the army. The British soldiers in a new trench were chatting, taking the lice from their uniforms, drinking tea and telling jokes.

'You are taking a risk, gentlemen,' the general said.

'We've been sent forward to observe the truce,' Silver Hand explained. 'To see the Germans lay down their arms and surrender.'

'I see,' the general said. 'No one told me you were coming.'

Grimm looked surprised. 'Really? A message was sent yesterday. I guess with this sudden cease-fire everything is a little confused.'

'It's been chaos the past few days,' the general agreed. He glanced at his wristwatch. 'Ten a.m. now. Can't you wait? The war ends at eleven.'

'Yes, but we have to be there... on the German side... for then. So if you don't mind, we'll cross no man's land now.'

The general's jaw went slack. 'Are you quite mad? They can still shoot you right up to the eleventh hour of the eleventh day of the eleventh month. Armistice doesn't start till then.'

Father Gaulle was getting restless. They'd spent the night before just five miles behind this front line and word was going around the soldiers' camp. The military police were looking for two men. Traitors. A sergeant with a metal hand and a Catholic priest. If they found them the men would stand trial and hang. If they tried to escape, the police had the right to shoot them down. But no one was looking for *two* priests and Grimm had hidden his metal hand in a glove. It was urgent that they get across to the safety of their homeland as soon as possible.

'You must have also missed the message which says the Germans have agreed not to shoot anyone who is showing a white flag.' He picked up a stick and tied a grubby white handkerchief to the end. 'This will do.'

The general shook his head. 'Sounds odd to me. But if you have your orders I'll have a look at them and let you take the risk.'

'Orders?' Gaulle said. 'Do you have the orders, Father?'

Grimm joined in the play-acting. 'I thought you had them. They're in my pack, but that's back at base camp, five miles away.'

'Oh dear, if the good general here sends us all the way back there'll be terrible trouble.'

A captain arrived with a thick pile of telegraph messages for the general. 'Orders for the day, sir.'

The general rubbed his tired eyes. He waved a hand at Grimm and Gaulle. 'Oh you'd better get away then. But I won't be to blame if they welcome you with machine guns.'

Sergeant Grimm almost saluted. 'Thank you, sir. When they see two priests they will not shoot. A sensible decision from you.'

He turned on his heel and marched to the steps that led up from the trench to the muddy patch of ground above.

The German trenches showed a line of sandbags. Sad soldiers looked over the top as Silver Hand and his friend waved their white flag and started to cross the half mile to safety. When they were over halfway across – a hundred yards from safety – Grimm called out in German, 'Greetings, comrades. *Hallo, kameraden.*'

The sullen and sulking German soldiers watched in silence.

* * *

A mile behind the German trenches the gunners were in a different mood. A man with a small moustache stood on a gun carriage and shouted, 'We didn't *lose* this war. *Traitors* back in Germany *threw* it away. *Traitors* who *starved* the German people so they could make *money* from selling food. First we will *destroy* the traitors. Then we will build *newer* and *better* guns and ships, planes and tanks, make *deadlier* gases and make sure every German is *fitter* to fight.'

The gunners cheered. But one man spoke against the man with the moustache. 'The British will be here in an hour. They'll take our guns away from us.'

'We'll make more,' someone argued and he was cheered too.

'They'll take our shells and turn them against us.'

'Then let's get rid of the shells. Let's fire them all.'

'If we hit the British trenches they'll start firing back. We'll all be killed. How stupid would that be?'

The man with the moustache waved a hand. 'I didn't say hit the trenches. Let the shells explode in no man's land. It will be one last fireworks party. Who agrees?'

It seemed as if the whole troop of gunners agreed. They ran laughing to their cannon and loaded them. When the man with the moustache waved his handkerchief they fired. The shells soared and landed in the muddy earth between the German and the British trenches. The British troops ducked out of sight and wondered at their enemy's final burst of madness.

Sergeant Grimm and Father Benedict were smiling and waving when the shells began to land. They struggled to go forward and couldn't go back.

When a shell explodes near a man he is not wounded. He is turned into vapour. He is scattered like a fine mist on a foggy November day.

One moment the men in the trenches were watching two priests struggle through the mud. The next there was nothing left of them.

They were gone, faster than the speed of life.

Nothing left? Almost nothing.

The hot steel of war had claimed its last victims before the silver hand of peace put an end to the cruelty.

Chapter Nine

'The name of peace is sweet'

11 November 1923: Hirson

The November day was cold but fine as the soldiers marched through the streets of Hirson. They paused at the stone cross in the market square and stood in silence to remember the friends who had died in the Great War. It was five years since the peace but the memories were still strong and bitter.

After a service of prayers and hymns and a speech from the mayor, the people made their way home with their memories of the dark days.

Some headed for the Blue Boar tavern for lunch. The quiet crowd was disturbed when the door banged open and a farmer stood there, red-faced from the cold and eyes shining with excitement. 'Landlord,' he cried. 'Tell me that story about the man with the silver hand.'

The man behind the bar poured a glass of wine and said, 'Settle down, Charles.'

The farmer gulped the wine and spoke quickly. 'Remember the story you told after the war. You said a man came in here – a British soldier with a Catholic priest. The soldier had a silver hand.'

'I remember,' the landlord nodded. The people in the bar were all listening now. 'He showed us his hand. He said he was a hero – he had rescued an officer under heavy machine-gun fire, but lost his hand. The officer was so thankful he paid to have a new hand made. It was made from the officer's family silver. It was solid metal and worth a fortune.'

'And what happened to the man with the silver hand?' Charles went on.

'He headed east and was never seen again. Maybe he died saving someone else. Maybe he went home safe.'

'No,' Charles chuckled. 'He died in my two-hectare field... the place where the Germans stopped and made peace.'

'How do you know that?' someone at the bar asked.

'Because I found what was left of him. I was ploughing the land and I turned over this.' He reached into his pocket. He paused. With all the drama of a stage actor he pulled out a shining silver hand. The crowd in the bar gave a sigh. 'I reckon it was on my land so it's mine. All that silver. I'm rich, lads. Rich.'

A shrunken man in a black coat spoke up. 'Let me have a look at it.'

'It's mine,' Charles said and clutched it to his mud-stained chest.

'Charles, you are too mean to ever buy jewels for your poor wife,' the landlord explained. 'So you won't know this is Mr Garde... he has been a jeweller for fifty years. He will tell you what it's worth.'

Charles slowly opened his hand and let the man take the metal hand. The jeweller's mouth turned down. He weighed it in his hand and took out an eyeglass so he could look closely at the scratches in the metal. 'My friend,' he said sadly. 'I do not need to test this. I can tell you it is not silver.'

'What is it?'

'Tin. Cheap tin.'

'What's it worth?'

'Nothing.'

The farmer sat down heavily on a chair. 'But the soldier's story...'

'A lie. The man was a liar. A fraud,' the jeweller said gently.

'The silver hand?' the farmer said.

'Give it to the town museum. It's a lie. A lie.'

Chapter Ten

'Friendship increases happiness, and reduces misery'

11 November 1923: Bray

Aimee Fletcher walked through the streets of Bray. She tried not to slip on the icy cobbles. The town was patched and mended now but the new bricks showed like fresh scars on old wounds. The town was repaired but not healed. There were blood-red poppies standing frosted on the war memorial. 11th November had been the day the town remembered the dead.

The children in the school had been told about the war that day. The youngest ones couldn't remember it. Even some of the older ones had forgotten what had happened five years before when they were so young.

But Aimee was able to tell them about war balloons, the aeroplanes and the famous Red Baron who had died so close to their town. She told them about the tanks and the gas, the refugees and the rain. The story of the White Lady group she told with pride; the story of the traitors, and Sergeant Grimm, she kept to herself.

The cat that was the colour of rust and ashes followed her up the lane to the farm. It was getting old now. It still sat guard at the school gates during the day but went back to the Fletcher farm with Aimee every night to sleep by the log fire.

Aimee's plaited hair was longer now and wrapped in a coil around her head. She wasn't the wild, pigtailed child any longer. Colette Fletcher stood at the door of the farmhouse with a broad smile to welcome her daughter home.

'What's wrong, Maman? Is father sick with the gas on his lungs again?'

'No, Aimee. It's a surprise. You have a guest.'

The girl entered the warm kitchen and took off her coat. Her guest sat by the fireplace, opposite her father. He had grown so much in the five years since they'd said goodbye, she hardly knew him.

'Hello, Marius,' she said.

He rose to his feet and she saw he was taller than her father now. They shook hands, stiff and awkward. 'You are still at school?' he asked, speaking good French.

Aimee threw back her head and laughed. 'Sort of. Master DuPont is getting too old so I help him with the teaching. He lives across the road from the school. He'd love to see you. Let's go down before it gets dark.'

'He saved our lives,' Marius said. 'A great man.'

As they hurried through the door Colette Fletcher called, 'Don't be too late, supper is in an hour. You're welcome to stay, Marius.'

And they were gone. Master DuPont was frail now and his silver-topped cane was used for walking, not clubbing traitors to the ground. They sat around his fire and lived again those months before the Armistice. 'And now, Marius?'

'I am a student. In three years' time I will be a doctor, I hope.'

Master DuPont and Aimee nodded. It was what they had hoped for too.

'And you will work in Germany. How are things there?'

Marius's face darkened in the flickering light of the fire. 'The war is not over,' he said quietly. 'So many men came home and said we weren't beaten by the enemy, we were beaten by traitors back at home. They say that in the next war we will root out the traitors and be stronger than ever.'

'The *next* war?' Aimee moaned. 'No, no, no. What about the silver hand of peace we used to talk about?'

'Not silver,' Marius said. 'No better than tin.'

'We'll be enemies again?' the girl sighed.

Marius looked at her and smiled. 'Enemies, never. When I am a doctor I am going to move to France to work. France needs doctors too.'

'You'll go to a great city like Paris or Rheims and make your fortune, I suppose,' Aimee said.

'No. I don't want to work for silver. I want to help the people we hurt in the war. People like your father with his gas-wrecked lungs. I was thinking of setting up a practice in a small town in France.'

'Which one?'

Mater DuPont said, 'I think I know the name of the town.'

Marius's smile became a grin. 'You are a clever man, Master DuPont. I think you may be right.'

'Are you going to tell me which town or leave me guessing?' the girl cried.

Marius and the teacher looked at one another. Then they turned to Aimee and said, together, 'Bray-on-Somme.'

And the warmth of friendship was warmer than the amber fire.

NOTES

Diphenylamine chlorarsine (DM)

DM gas was invented by an American scientist called Major Robert Adams and was stockpiled by both Britain and the United States at the end of World War I. It would put enemy soldiers out of action without killing them. German gas masks would be useless. The war ended before it was ever used.

Manfred von Richthofen

Manfred von Richthofen (2 May 1892 – 21 April 1918) was known as the Red Baron, and was a German fighter pilot during the First World War. He shot down more enemy aircraft than anyone. He arrived at Bray with seventy victories. He added ten more before he was shot down and killed near Bray. He was almost certainly shot by a soldier on the ground.

Bray-on-Somme

The German army entered Bray in late August 1914 and in the first month the town was not too badly disturbed. The British fought back with heavy bombing, and forced the Germans to leave on 4th October 1914. For the next twenty-eight months Bray was used as an important rest centre for the French army. On 21st March 1918 the Germans launched an attack named Operation Michael, while Bray was held by the British army. On 26th March the desperate British army managed to hold back the enemy with the help of twelve of the first Whippet tanks to be used in action. But in the end Bray was given up without a fight. For the next four months the Germans used Bray as a base. Again French and British forces bombed the town. The German forces were weak from the flu epidemic. On 24th August 1918 a Canadian force drove them out.

For its four years of suffering during the Great War the town of Bray was awarded the *Croix de Guerre* (Cross of War) by the French in 1920. The town was rebuilt over many years.

Bray was occupied by the Germans from 1940 to 1944 during the Second World War. On 1st September 1944, Bray was set free by the United States army.

Today Bray Museum shows memories of the Great War. Manfred von Richthofen, the Red Baron, is remembered along with his squadron, the 'Flying Circus'.